CLAIMING HER MATES: BOOK ONE

DIA COLE

Claiming Her Mates: Book One

Published by Black Diamond Press LLC.

Cover Art by Addendum Designs

Edited by Anne-Marie Rutella

ISBN: 978-1-946975-20-1

Three Lykos shifters swore to protect Havana. But who will protect them from her?

With everyone bailing on my holiday party, I didn't think the night could get any worse. Then three scorching hot men storm the club and demand I come with them. Thinking they're cops, I run only to discover the flu vaccine is turning people into monsters.

Now my survival depends on Mason, Gabriel, and Liam. I should be terrified of their glowing eyes and the way they destroy any threat in our path, but all I can think about is claiming the fierce men as my own. All three of them...

One problem.

My ex has threatened to eviscerate any man who touches me. Too bad the deadly Alpha male isn't here. He'll rue the day he broke my heart and ordered his three gorgeous friends to rescue me.

For the brothers...

❦ I ❦

HAVANA

"What do you want for Christmas, you naughty girl?" asked the middle-aged man leering at me. The light from the dusty chandelier reflected off the gold band on his left hand, temporarily blinding me.

He probably told his wife he was working late. Ugh. Years of playing my seductive role prevented me from curling my lip in disdain. Instead, I continued undulating to the beat of the dance music being piped into the small red velvet VIP room.

"Come on, you can tell me," the man insisted, stroking his Santa-like white beard.

I should've been coy with my answer, but the truth sprang from my lips before I could bite back the words. "Someone to share it with."

The man blinked up at me with blood-shot eyes.

Great, Vana, why don't you just kill the mood? Trying to salvage the moment, I tossed back my hip-length black hair and winked playfully. "Is that someone you?" With a practiced flick of my fingers, I slowly removed my silver-studded black top and tossed it to the man.

He tried to catch it and missed. The tiny scrap of material

slithered to the blood-red carpet as he fixed his gaze on my swaying bare breasts.

"Have you been a bad boy this year?"

"Y-yes," he stammered. His eyes glazed over as he swayed in his seat.

He must be trashed. Good. A drunk and his money are soon parted. Throwing club rules out the window, I stepped down from the small raised platform I was dancing on and approached his chair. "Then you need to be punished."

"Yes, Mistress Robin," he gasped. Unlike most of the club patrons intrigued by my dominatrix persona, this one seemed truly snared by the fantasy. For the right price, I was happy to indulge him.

I cast a furtive glance at the camera nestled at the base of the chandelier. In the past, Max, the club owner, might've skinned me alive if he'd caught me doing a little extra on the side. Now he'd only ask for a percentage.

Times were tough for everyone. Strip clubs included. Case in point, this guy managed to secure a private dance from me for a mere seventy bucks, something that would've been unheard of before the canine flu hit this past spring. But global pandemics had a way of changing things.

I leaned over the man, my nipples grazing his rumpled tweed vest. "It'll cost you."

"I have money." He reached into his olive dress pants pocket and pulled out a worn leather wallet with trembling hands. "How much?"

I arched an eyebrow. "How much do you have?"

He opened his wallet and out fluttered several receipts.

Sadly, it looked like he had only a handful of twenties, but it was better than going home broke. "That works," I purred. I wouldn't have sex with him, of course, but men like him weren't after that anyway. Years ago, my mom explained some men get off as much on pain and humiliation as they did pleasure. Ah, the joys of having a stripper mom. While other kids were learning how to ride bikes, Mom was giving me crash courses in the various ways to seduce men. Big surprise I ended up at the same club where she used to work.

The man swallowed hard, sweat dripping off him as if he was in a sauna. "Take it all." He pushed his wallet at me.

I found myself staring at a family photo. Gathered in the arms of a heavyset woman were three young children. I couldn't help glancing between the professor and the photo. *Why isn't he home with them?* Hell, if I'd had kids there's no way I wouldn't be with them right now. With a pang, I remembered the big amber eyes of the little girl I'd used to nanny for. *I miss Mira so much...*

Her father's handsome face flashed in my mind and my throat tightened. It'd been three months since Nathan shattered my heart, but the pain was still fresh. Trying to put my ex out of my mind, I flipped past the photo and found the twenties. Mentally tallying the money, I pulled out the folded bills and slid them into the top of my thigh-high stiletto boot. A genuine smile tugged at the corner of my lips, it was a better haul than I'd anticipated. "Take off your clothes, Dr. Sullivan."

He gaped at me for a moment.

I tossed his wallet back at him not bothering to explain that I'd seen his Southern Arizona University ID badge inside. "I said, take off your clothes. Now."

He jumped to his feet. "Yes, Mistress Robin." He gazed up at me adoringly.

My five-foot-ten height plus my seven-inch stilettos ensured I towered over nearly everyone I encountered, including the professor.

He fumbled with the top buttons of his oxford shirt before realizing he needed to remove his vest first.

"Fold your clothes and place them over there," I

instructed, pointing at the side table that in better days held ice buckets filled with Cristal. Now a bottle of drugstore champagne swam in a plastic tub of melted ice.

He practically tore off his vest and shirt. As he unbuckled his belt, he turned to face me. "I've never done this before."

I made a noncommittal noise. *Right. That's what they all say*. Finally noticing his bare torso, I inhaled sharply. *What the hell?* Black veins covered the man's flabby arms and a portion of his silver-haired chest. I'd seen some strange-looking tattoos over the years, but nothing like that. Unable to help myself, I asked, "What's going on there?"

The man looked down and paled. "My God. Those weren't there this morning." He gave me a frantic look as if I had the answers.

I backed up a step studying his bloodshot eyes, pale skin, and sweaty face with new eyes. *He's not just drunk.* "You're sick." And that meant I needed to get as far away from him as possible. I'd never heard of the canine flu causing dark veins like that, but you don't mess around with a bug that killed a quarter of the world's population.

He raised his hands. "I'm not. I just got the canine flu vaccine yesterday," he said, mentioning the coveted shots the CDC had just rolled out. "I-I don't feel so good." His knees buckled, and he fell back into his chair.

Shit. "I'll get help." *Max will know what to do.* I turned to grab the curtain.

"No. My wife. She can't find out..." he gasped sliding to the floor.

Damn. If the guy passed out in my VIP room, I'd never hear the end of it from the other girls. Especially Jess. That nasty redhead would love to get one over on me. She'd been downright venomous since I reported one of her stupid pranks to Max. *Who the hell coats the stage steps with baby oil? Seriously.* I'd taken a nasty fall and probably fractured my spine, not that I could afford to get my aching back looked at by a doctor.

"Please, don't call Sharon," the professor wheezed bringing my focus back to him.

"No one will call your wife. Just relax. I'll be right back." I bent down, retrieved my top and tied it back on.

He nodded, flashing me a relieved look.

I blinked. *Are more of his veins darkening?* Shuddering, I pushed through the heavy velvet curtain door and rushed down a long hallway back into the main club. Immediately I was assaulted by the smell of liquor, cigarette smoke, and the twang of the latest hit country single. On the stage, the new girl, Jade, twirled around the pole in a cowboy hat and crotchless chaps. *Poor girl,* I thought with a stab of sympathy. Max had wanted me to cover Jess's country set after she was a no-show for the second time this week, but I'd talked him into having the new girl do it. Good experience and all. Seeing her dance to a sea of empty tables filled me with guilt. No one even watched. Sly, one of the regulars, was already passed out and the group of dark-haired men sitting in the back of the club ignored her.

As if feeling my gaze, one of the heavily tattooed men looked up at me. He gave me a once-over and flashed me a dazzling set of gold teeth. The long-haired man sitting next to him followed his friend's gaze and leered at me with a predatory intensity that made me glad for the knife hidden in my boot. A girl couldn't be too careful these days.

I bit back a shiver of fear as the long-haired man beckoned me over. Their gang, the Calaveras, was one of the deadliest in Arizona and I needed their kind of attention like I needed an engineering degree. Ignoring the men and their menacing vibe, I scanned the rest of the near empty club for Max.

He was at the bar, eyes glued to the television along with

Donna, the cocktail waitress, and Justin, the gray-haired bartender who looked like he'd been a defensive lineman back in the day. I'd always wondered why he had a television at his bar. *I mean who comes to a strip club to watch TV?*

Donna looked up as I approached. "Honey, you need to see this. There's some freaky shit going down." She ran a hand through her bleach blond hair, knocking aside the felt Santa hat she was wearing.

I shook my head. "Tell me about it. I got a guy covered in black veins about to pass out in the VIP room."

"What?" Max jerked his bald head up so fast his jowls shook.

"We might need to call an ambulance." I waited for Max to make an obscene joke, but instead a panicked expression crossed his face.

"You said his veins were black?"

I nodded.

Donna let out a gasp. "The news reporter said to watch out for people with dark veins. Some folks are having bad reactions to the canine flu vaccine. They're getting sick and..." she lowered her voice, "turning into cannibals."

I gave her an incredulous look. "What?"

"See for yourself." She waved at the television hanging above a tower of colorful liquor bottles.

On the screen a flustered news reporter was babbling. "Reports of violent behavior in some of the recently vaccinated are coming in from all across the country."

The program cut to a clip of dazed-looking people in hospital gowns attacking a young man on the street. The jerky footage must've been taken on someone's cell phone. Whoever was holding the phone kept repeating, "Holy shit," over and over while the crowd literally tore the screaming man to pieces.

My stomach churned as I watched the deranged crowd

gulp down handfuls of the man's flesh. "That's horrible. I can't believe they showed that on television."

Donna shook her head. "It's not just happening here. It's happening all over the world. They rushed the flu vaccine to market without doing the proper tests and now it's turning people into monsters. Oh, God. And just an hour ago I was cursing the fact that they didn't have the vaccine available for Gavin." She let out a sob at the mention of her son who'd died of the flu earlier in the year.

"Don't cry, muffin," Max said in a gruff voice. He slung one beefy arm around Donna's thin shoulder and gave me a hard look. "Get that sick guy out of here. Now." He used his don't-argue-with-me voice.

That tone hadn't worked on me since I'd been ten. "But Max—"

He interrupted me. "I'll call him a cab. You get him in it. We're closing early tonight. Donna, go get Sly up. I'll tell Mr. Diaz and his men that they need to leave." He looked over at the dark-haired men in back and shuddered. "Let's hope they don't kill me," he muttered under his breath as he headed over to their table.

I'd take the sick professor over throwing deadly gang members out of the club any day. As I turned to walk back to the VIP area, Donna called my name softly.

I spun around to see that the older woman wore an anxious expression on her face.

She smoothed an invisible wrinkle from her short black skirt. "Honey, I'm sorry but Max and I won't be able to make your Christmas Eve dinner."

"Oh," I said, trying not to let my disappointment show. *You and everyone else.* "That's too bad."

"We're sorry to miss it, it's just that with everything going on..." She waved weakly at the television set. "And it's our first Christmas without Gavin." Her voice hitched.

"I understand." I reached over and hugged her. I missed that kid something fierce. Pushing the memory of the mischievous little boy out of my mind before I started tearing up too, I looked over at Justin. "You and Sam are still coming, right?"

The big guy shook his head. "Sorry, sweetheart. Sam just wants to do a family thing this year." He gave me an apologetic smile.

Family thing. Right. "Well, more turkey for me," I said, hiding my misery with a smile. "Have a good night."

Donna and Justin waved as I headed back toward the professor. My chest tightened. Bad enough that the anniversary of my mother's death was Christmas Eve. Now I'd have to endure it alone.

The wail of country music faded as I moved past the stage and through the long, deserted hallway. I stopped at the closed velvet curtain to the room where I'd left the professor. A low moaning sound came from inside. "Dr. Sullivan?" I reached out to pull open the curtain and hesitated. I'd never realized how far from the main club this area was. *What if the professor is sick like the people on TV? What if he attacks me?*

❋   2   ❋

HAVANA

A large hand clamped down on my shoulder.

A shriek lodged in my throat as I spun around and came face-to-face with two tall, muscular men.

The shorter man, if you could call a man over six feet short, offered me a dazzling, panty-dropping smile. "Sorry to startle you, love."

The man's sexy English accent paired with tousled blond hair and ocean-blue eyes had me returning his smile and flipping back my hair. "No harm, no foul. How can I help you?"

The other man stepped forward. His six-foot-four height put me at eye level with the black eye patch over his right eye. The patch combined with his five o'clock shadow and collar-length hair gave him a definite bad-boy vibe that made my blood hum.

"We're here for you," tall dark and handsome said in a deep voice.

Holy hotness. I'll stay after hours for these guys. I licked my lips feeling my hormones wake for the first time in months. "If you want to step into a room—" I gestured to the open rooms down the hall "—I'll be right there."

Tall dark and handsome frowned. "You misunderstand. Havana, you need to come with us right now."

The sound of my real name had me staring at the two men in shocked silence for half a second. "Do I know you?" *Have I danced for them before? No.* I'd definitely remember men this good-looking.

The clean-shaven blond, who looked like a *GQ* model, shook his head. He wore khakis and a blue polo shirt under his jacket, which matched the stunning hue of his eyes perfectly. "I'm Mason Wheeler and he's Gabriel Perez."

I looked over at the dark-haired man whose black clothing and golden complexion almost made me mistake him for one of the Calaveras. But there was no way I would've missed his eye patch and smoldering good looks among the gang members.

Why are they here for me? There was only one plausible explanation. "Are you guys cops?"

The two men exchanged a look.

Fucking A. And I didn't think my night could get any worse. My stomach sank and my mind raced as I tried to think of a reason the cops would want to talk to me. "Is this about the Strip Club Killer?" My throat tightened as I remembered how close I'd come to joining his victims.

"No," Gabriel said.

Okay. Then what? "Look, I pay my taxes." Maybe I didn't always report every tip, but enough.

Mason's sinfully full lips quirked up. "This isn't about your taxes."

Damn, these were the sexiest cops I'd ever seen. I almost wanted them to arrest me. *Maybe this is about the internet stuff?* I folded my arms over my chest. "Last time I checked being a cam girl wasn't illegal and—"

Gabriel cleared his throat interrupting me. "Enough. We're running out of time." He stepped forward and stared into my eyes. "Ms. James, come with us now." His voice rang with a strange tone.

Rubbing my temple where my head suddenly ached, I said, "Don't I have a right to an attorney and a phone call?"

Gabriel's mouth fell open as if I'd shocked him.

"Mistress Robin," the professor wheezed from the VIP room. "I think I need to see a doctor."

Gabriel stepped by me, slid open the curtain, and cursed. "It's one of the infected."

I peered around his muscular shoulder and found the professor slumped on the floor with his shirt in his lap. There were even more dark veins running across his chest. "Can you get your shirt on, Dr. Sullivan?" I asked with a calmness I didn't feel. "Max is calling you a cab. You can take it straight to the hospital. We can call an ambulance if you want..."

"No. A cab is fine. Thank you." The professor slowly pulled on his shirt with shaking hands. In that moment, he looked old and frail.

Feeling sorry for the man, I reached into the top of my boot and pulled out his money. "You can have this back since we didn't—"

"Move away from him," Gabriel said, grabbing my arm. "He's infected with the virus."

"The virus?" I echoed. *Is he talking about the canine flu?*

"Keep the money," the professor said with a wan smile. "It can be a holiday advance. I'll come back and collect my... punishment when I'm feeling better."

"Thank you," I replied, not knowing what else to say.

Gabriel tugged my elbow. "Come on. This way." He pulled me toward the main part of the club.

I caught a whiff of his scent—smoke and leather. The dark masculine smell made my insides tighten.

Mason fell into step beside us. "We're parked out front."

Sandwiched between the two hot men, my knees weakened. *Maybe I can ask them to handcuff me?* I quickly bitch slapped my libido. *Get a grip, Vana.* It figured the first men I'd be attracted to since my breakup with Nathan would be cops wanting to question me.

We'd almost passed the side stairs to the dressing room when I remembered my things. I stopped short, dragging Gabriel back a step. "I need to change." No way was I going to walk into a police station in my dance outfit. Besides, I didn't want to leave the rest of my money here where it could grow legs and walk out of my locker before my next shift.

Mason let go of my arm. "Okay."

Gabriel frowned. "We don't have time—"

"Couldn't we spare her a minute?" Mason asked, interrupting the taller man.

I beamed at the blond, deciding I liked him more than his gruff partner.

Gabriel gritted his teeth and nodded. "Just one minute."

Relieved, I rushed up the stairs. When the men tried to follow me, I held out my hand to stop them. "You can't come back here." Max was the only guy allowed in the dressing room and it was only because he barreled his way in like a bull whenever he felt like it.

"Hurry," Gabriel ordered, looking down at his watch.

Wondering what crawled up his butt and died, I headed backstage and made a beeline for the empty dressing room.

It wasn't much, just a row of vanity mirrors and a bank of lockers. I went straight to my locker and pulled out the duffel bag that held my purse, makeup, toiletries, spare dance outfits, the wad of ones I'd milked out of the professor earlier in the night, and most important, the bottle of pain pills my back would soon be begging for. I quickly chewed the pills and dry swallowed down their bitter taste.

After throwing a skintight black dress over my skimpy dance outfit, I shrugged into my long charcoal wool jacket.

My aching feet pleaded with me to ditch my boots, but I'd neglected to bring other shoes.

My cell rang as I was closing my locker door. I answered it to the shriek of my roommate, Sydney.

"I can't believe you talked me into this, Vana!"

"What?" I drew a blank for a moment before remembering she was covering a private party for me. "Are you at that bachelor's party?"

"I'm hiding in a freaking stranger's closet wearing nothing but a thong and some pasties."

I couldn't help laughing. "There are worse ways of making two hundred bucks."

"You know how I hate dark, cramped spaces. I owe you big-time for this."

"Yeah, like twenty percent," I reminded her. Thinking of how little I'd made tonight, I sighed. *Serves me right for ditching that job in favor of Max's request to work late tonight.* Family before work, I would've reminded myself if he and Donna hadn't just bowed out of the one event I asked them to attend all year.

"It smells like mothballs in here," Sydney said, returning my focus to our phone call. "This has to be the worst night ever."

"At least you don't have two cops waiting to take you down to the station."

She gasped. "What? Why?"

"I don't know."

"Crap, girl. Are you in trouble? Do you need me to blow this gig? I could—"

"No, you stay in that closet," I said with a tight laugh. "You need the money. *We* need the money. Besides, they aren't arresting me." *At least right now.* I looked down at my bag, unzipped it, and reluctantly put the pain pills back in my locker. Back pain or no back pain, I couldn't afford to get busted with illegal meds. "And they're the hottest cops you've ever seen."

"Hot enough to make you forget about that asshole Nathan?"

Not this again. I rolled my eyes already anticipating the lecture.

Syd took a deep breath. "I know he was rich as Midas and gorgeous as hell, but Nathan was also a cheating son of a bitch. It's been three months since you two broke up. Time to get back in the saddle."

"Right," I said, agreeing to end the conversation. There was no point in me trying to explain heartbreak to someone who'd never been in love.

"You need to promise me you'll give the next guy who goes after you a chance."

"And what if the next guy is Phil?"

She laughed. "Okay, obviously not our pervy neighbor. But you know what I mean."

Knowing she could be as tenacious as a Gila monster when she set her mind to something, I sighed. "I promise. Look, I've got to go, but I'll text you when I figure out what's going on."

"Okay. I'm heading right to the airport for my red-eye after this, but I'll call you as soon as I land."

"Have a safe flight," I said feeling a stab of envy that she had parents and siblings to share the holidays with. It seemed everyone had a family, but me.

Jade walked through the dressing room door just as I hung up the phone. "Heading out?" she asked with a sniff. Her heavily kohled eyes swam with tears.

Now, she's definitely having a worse night than us. "Are you okay?" I didn't know much about the green-haired woman other than she'd started last night.

She pressed her trembling lips together and shook her head.

Damn. I'd been there before. Setting down my bag, I walked over to her side and put my hand on her shoulder. "It's not always like this you know. There are good nights and bad nights." *Just more bad nights lately.* "Things will pick up after the holidays." *I hope.*

Her expression crumbled. "I didn't make jack tonight."

Anxiety ate at me as I glanced at the empty doorway. I'd already made the cops wait far longer than a minute. Torn between the need to comfort the girl and the need not to piss off the officers who might hold my fate in their hands, I chewed my lower lip.

Jade let out a loud sob.

Screw it. The cops can wait. I led Jade to the nearest swivel chair. She sat, her chest heaving. "I'm sorry. I'm such a mess." She swiped a hand across her face, smearing her makeup. "I never thought it'd come to this. Me taking off my clothes for money. And when I finally get desperate enough to do it, I don't make a fucking cent." Tears trekked down her face. She was an ugly-crier, something that made me like her even more.

"It'll be okay," I said squeezing her shoulder. Desperation drove a lot of girls to dancing. Me included.

Jade let out a heavy sigh. "I thought for sure I'd make some good money. I'm so broke I can't even pay the sitter."

"You have kids?" I asked, grabbing a tissue from the counter and handing it to her.

She gave me a watery smile. "Payton just turned two."

My chest tightened. I was a sucker for little ones. Forbidding me from seeing Mira had to be one of the cruelest things Nathan could have done after breaking up with me.

I gave Jade a once-over. She was pretty in that girl-next-door kind of way. With the right makeup and outfit she'd kill it. "Look, how about I give you some pointers tomorrow night?"

Her raccoon eyes widened as she studied my face. "Seriously?"

"Until then, take this." I fished out two twenties and gave them to her.

Her eyes widened and then narrowed. "For real?" Like most of us, she'd probably been kicked around by life to the point she had a hard time believing that anyone would do something nice for no reason.

"Yeah, consider it a welcome-to-the-club present. I was new once too, and I barely made anything my first night," I said, lying. "I'm Havana, by the way." I held out my hand to her.

She shook it. "Melody."

"Nice to meet you, Melody. Now don't waste any more tears on this shithole. Go home and enjoy your baby."

She smiled for the first time. "I will."

I walked back over to my bag and slung the strap over my shoulder. As I walked through the doorway, I stopped and said, "Hey, if you and Payton aren't doing anything Christmas Eve you're welcome to come to my place. I cook a mean turkey with all the sides."

She blinked up at me. "Thanks, but we're going to my sister's."

Of course. It was destined to be me and me alone this Christmas. "Well, I'd better not keep those cops waiting any longer. See you tomorrow assuming they don't throw me in jail."

She blinked. "You mean the pirate-looking guy and the hot blond that came in a little while ago?"

"Yeah."

"They aren't cops."

I whirled around. "What do you mean?"

She dabbed her eye with the tissue. "My stepdad was a sergeant with SVPD before he died. If there is one thing I know, it's law enforcement and those guys aren't it. Not by a long shot."

My stomach dropped to the floor as I looked toward the side stairs. *If Mason and Gabriel weren't cops, who were they? And what did they want with me?*

❈ 3 ❈

MASON

Gabriel glowered. "We're wasting time. There's a goddamn apocalypse happening if you hadn't noticed."

I shook my head at the ornery male. His mood was surlier than ever. "The female just wanted to get dressed." Although to be honest, I'd prefer she didn't. I peered through the darkness in the direction the woman had gone. My inhuman eyes quickly adjusted to the dim light allowing me to see the empty backstage area as if hundred-watt bulbs illuminated it. Unfortunately, it gave me no glimpses of the lovely Havana.

Just imagining her peeling away that tiny black number made me catch my breath.

What a magnificent creature she was from her slumberous dark eyes, to her generous breasts, to her long legs that I couldn't help but imagine wrapped around my hips. Even the exotic sweetness of her scent was intoxicating. If I never saw the female again, her smell would be branded inside the marrow of my bones for the rest of my days.

I looked down at my shaking hands. *Odd.* It'd been years since I'd reacted like this to a female. Although to be honest, spending twenty-hour days at the hospital didn't lend itself to commingling with the opposite sex. However, commingling was something I very much wanted to do with Havana and maybe more. Like every Lykos male, I dreamed of finding the female who would claim me forever.

"Get a hold of yourself," Gabriel snarled into my mind.

I growled at his mental intrusion. Although speaking telepathically was an ability of our species, it was considered rude to read another's thoughts. Not that Gabriel cared about offending an Omega like me. As the head Enforcer, the lethal Beta male did whatever he pleased and there wasn't a damn thing I could do about it.

"She's a human," he said in a chiding voice.

"Is she? You weren't able to compel her to come with us." I hadn't missed the Enforcer's attempt at compulsion. The strongest members of our species could compel weaker Lykos and humans to do their bidding. Sadly, I lacked that ability.

"She must be an Atavus," Gabriel muttered more to himself than to me.

I nodded in agreement. Given her resistance to his compulsion, it was highly likely she had a Lykos ancestor. Over the years, inbreeding between Lykos and humans resulted in distant generations that carried dormant Lykos genes in their DNA. Although they didn't shift or have many of our other abilities, their Lykos genes made them stronger than normal humans and more resistant to compulsion. It also made them very attractive to our species. Very attractive indeed. I glanced back over at the stairs willing the lovely Havana to reappear.

"She belongs to Nathan," Gabriel growled.

Bloody hell. A sharp ache flashed through me at the reminder the female was off-limits. *Why didn't I find her before Nathan did?* I gritted my teeth. *Is she his mate? No.* Alphas didn't take mates and even if they did, humans and Atavus didn't mate with our kind. Well, not in the share-a-lifelong-bond-until-death kind of way. However, there was nothing preventing our kind from enjoying the pleasures of their flesh. Something I'd never been tempted to do. *Until now.*

Gabriel scowled. "She's a complication we don't need. Especially now. I don't know what Nathan is thinking sending us after her."

I took a deep breath and brought my thoughts back under control. "It's not our place to question the Alphas." The Alphas gave the orders, and we followed. Something I'd discovered the hard way when Tasha, the ruthless Alpha female who ran our faction, educated me on the natural order of our species. I swallowed down the bitter taste in my mouth.

"Don't I know it," snapped Gabriel.

I couldn't help glancing at his eye patch. Not for the first time, I wondered what he'd done to warrant Tasha's cruel punishment.

Gabriel paced back and forth in front of the red velvet curtain. "Tasha ordered me to bring you and Nathan back to Winterhaven ASAP. If that doesn't happen..." His expression darkened.

Thud.

We both looked over at the red curtain.

"What the...?" Gabriel swiped the curtain open.

The infected human male was lying prone on the ground. Based on his shallow breathing, he was not long for this world. The faint pulse of his carotid artery seemed to flutter along with the beat of the music coming from the speakers on the wall.

I fisted my hands, torn between wanting to help and wanting to get the hell away from him as quickly as possible.

"There's nothing you can do," Gabriel reminded me.

That wasn't entirely true. I reached for the syringe in my

jacket pocket. I hadn't tested this substrain of the antivirus yet. So far my research had been confined to samples of the Z-virus in petri dishes. Conducting a human trial without thorough testing went against my medical ethics.

The human moaned again.

Screw ethics. I might be this man's only chance. And if it worked, we'd have a proven cure to stop the spread of the virus before it destroyed all humanity. Filled with resolve, I ran over to the human and grabbed his arm. Frantically, I searched for a vein that wasn't necrotic.

"What are you doing?" Gabriel asked as I slid the needle into the human's cephalic vein.

"Trying to save him," I murmured, pressing the plunger. Injecting directly into the bloodstream would disperse the antivirus faster than an intramuscular injection and right now time was of the essence.

Gabriel pointed at the dark veins covering the man's arms and chest. "Is that from the vaccine?"

"Yes. The necrosis likely originated at the shoulder, that's where the vaccine was given." *Bloody hell. Why hadn't the CDC extensively tested the vaccine before distributing it?* "Hopefully, this works."

Gabriel watched me with narrowed eyes. "I thought there wasn't a cure."

"There isn't one yet, but I've been experimenting with the blood of our species. We're immune to this virus, like all viruses, and if we could confer that immunity to humans—"

"Our blood is poison to humans," Gabriel interrupted.

As if I didn't already know that. "I've been working to suppress the toxicity of our blood while enhancing the immune—" I broke off as the human on the floor convulsed. Panic gripped me. "No!"

The man let out a bloodcurdling cry. Blood poured out of his eyes, nose, and mouth—the signature reaction to Lykos blood poisoning. With a loud shuddering gasp, the human went still. He didn't draw another breath.

Regret pounded through me as I looked down at the empty syringe. "I killed him." *Damn it*. I never should've attempted a live trial. *I've just robbed this man of several hours of life*. With a curse, I threw the syringe across the small room.

In a rare show of empathy, Gabriel rested his hand on my shoulder. "He was already dead. If anything you put an end to his suffering."

There was truth to his words. The last stages of the Z-virus were devastating and at least I'd saved this man that harrowing fate. Letting out a deep breath, I pushed myself to my feet and followed Gabriel out of the room.

A deep rumbling voice called out from down the hallway, "Gabe, what's going on? I thought we were doing a quick in and out. Where's the female?"

I glanced up at the massive seven-foot-tall bearded giant whose broad shoulders skimmed both sides of the hallway. "Havana is changing."

Gabriel scowled at the other Enforcer. "You're supposed to wait in the car, Liam."

"I thought you might've run into trouble."

"The only trouble is the female is taking too long." Gabriel scowled at me.

"I'm sure she'll be here shortly." I turned to face the side stairs. Although I'd just met her, my blood hummed in anticipation of seeing her again. Her beautiful face could ease the sting of failing to save the infected human.

Liam cleared his throat. "You don't think she'll run, do you?"

She won't run. Will she? Maybe it wasn't the best idea to let her think we were cops. I swallowed hard imagining Nathan's reaction if we let her slip through our fingers. Getting on the wrong side of an Alpha was deadly. Even worse, we'd have lost one of the most captivating females I'd ever encountered. *It's too dangerous for her out there on her own.* "She'll be here in a minute," I stated with more confidence than I felt. *Bloody hell. What if she runs?*

Liam must've picked up on my worry. He straightened his thick shoulders. "There's a back exit that leads to the alley. I'll watch it."

"Good idea," Gabriel said with a relieved look.

Liam nodded and stomped back down the hallway toward the front of the club.

A gurgling sound came from the private room.

Gabriel and I whipped around to see the human stagger to his feet. A new scent wafted off the man—the sickly odor of death.

A sinking feeling hit my stomach. *I should've anticipated this.*

The human's eyes snapped open revealing cloudy white irises that fixed on my face. Its lack of heartbeat and the fact it no longer drew breath made it clear it was one of the reanimated. Although how it could possibly exist baffled me along with the rest of the medical community.

"It's one of them now," I said over the sound of the man's chattering teeth.

Gabriel cursed.

The creature sniffed the air in a decidedly canine-like way.

"Do they use smell to hunt like we do?" Gabriel asked in a low voice.

"It appears so." My exposure to the creatures was limited to the blood samples I'd worked with, the reports I'd been getting from other doctors and nurses, and the handful of restrained infected I'd dealt with in the hospital.

The creature staggered in our direction.

The impossibility of it fascinated me. "Look at how it ambulates without a working respiratory system, limbic system, or any functioning organs. Despite limited cortical activity, this man is... to put it in lay terms...deader than a doornail. And yet, look how it walks and hunts."

Gabriel gave me a dry look. "Do you want to make out with it, or do you want me to kill it?"

"It needs to be put down." Based on what'd I learned so far about the reanimated, they'd attack and try to consume any living creature until they experienced significant cerebral damage.

"I'll take care of it." Gabriel pulled out a gun, screwed on a sound suppressor, and shot the creature in the middle of the chest.

The reanimated man continued staggering forward seemingly unaware of the fist-sized hole in the center of its torso.

Gabriel fired several more body shots.

That won't do anything. "Shoot it in the head."

"Well, why didn't you say so?" Gabriel switched aim and pulled the trigger again.

At nearly point-blank range, the bullet took out the back of the creature's skull and its brains splattered nearly every surface of the red room.

I jumped back before reminding myself that we were immune to the virus. Still, we didn't need infected blood and skull fragments on our clothes when we were about to take a trip with the female. I looked over at the side stairs both relieved and disappointed not to see Havana there.

Gabriel snapped the curtain closed, hiding the grisly scene. Then he cocked his head as if listening for the club's reactions to the muffled sound of gunfire. Seemingly assured that no one heard anything over the sound of the music, he turned to me and said, "The female's five minutes are up. Where is she?"

❦ 4 ❦

HAVANA

"It's time to go," a deep voice boomed from beyond the dressing room.

Another male voice called out, "Havana, are you ready?"

It's them. I froze. Thinking back on my conversation with the guys, neither of them actually said they were cops. *Crap, I'm such an idiot.* They could be serial killers for all I knew.

"Jeez. You're white as a ghost. Are you okay?" Jade asked in a concerned voice.

"Yeah, I'm fine," I said with confidence I didn't feel. "See you tomorrow night." I gave her a wave and walked through the doorway into the backstage area of the club. For a moment I debated going straight to Max. He and Justin would run the guys off the property in a heartbeat, but I hated the idea of bringing drama to work especially when Max had his hands full dealing with the Calaveras.

Deciding to ditch the guys for now, I rushed over to the side exit. Hopefully, I'd be halfway home before Gabriel and Mason even noticed I was gone. Bracing myself for the chill,

I shoved open the door, and stepped out into the dimly lit alley.

The rancid odor of urine, rotting garbage, and a tangy metallic scent I couldn't place engulfed me. *Ugh. Now I remember why I don't go out this way.* Besides the creep factor of trekking through a dark alley alone, the stench was enough to peel the flesh from my bones. My breath fogged the air in front of my face while I struggled not to lose the salad I'd had for dinner.

Click. Click. Click.

What's that? Swallowing back nausea, I peered down the alley.

Three figures lurched around an overflowing Dumpster. The weird chittering sound seemed to be coming from them.

Initially, I dismissed the trio as homeless Dumpster divers. Then they moved into the light.

I gasped in recognition. It was Jess, along with her drug-dealing boyfriend, Brody. But they didn't look right. The light from the parking lot illuminated their strange white eyes and the crimson stains around their gnashing teeth. Limping next to them was an unfamiliar short guy who was missing half his face. His one remaining eye swung from his socket like a lost headphone.

They're like the crazy people on the news!

Shit! Deciding it'd be better to take my chances with Gabriel and Mason, I grabbed for the club door handle. It wouldn't open.

The three of them staggered closer.

My heart pounded like a kettledrum. "Stay back!" I pulled the folding knife from my boot and flicked out the blade.

Jess let out a low moan. Intestines spilled out of the front of her yellow dress and swung from side to side like tentacles as she tottered toward me in platform heels.

Oh, God! If being disemboweled hadn't stopped her, my four-inch knife sure as hell wasn't going to be a deterrent. Fear turned my blood into ice as I turned and raced down the alley as fast as I could in my stiletto boots. The parking lot was in sight when the biggest man I'd ever seen in my life stepped into the alley ahead of me. *Shit!* I stopped so suddenly, the heel of my right boot snapped off and I flew forward.

As I slammed onto the ground, the knife sliced into my palm. I muffled a cry focusing not on the pain, but on the hulking man ahead of me.

The giant's massive shoulders blocked out the light as he let out a growl that made every hair on my body stand on end. Impossibly, his eyes seemed to glow in the darkness.

Oh, God! Monsters in front. Monsters behind. Terror paralyzed me, and the knife fell out of my bleeding hand. The frenzied chattering of teeth grew louder and louder until it seemed to rattle my bones. A rush of adrenaline had me stumbling to my feet. Hearing a low moan, I twisted around just in time to see Brody launch himself at me.

Damn it. He wasn't as big as the giant, but his lanky six-foot frame knocked into me like a wrecking ball. As I fell onto the ground, pain radiated out from my back.

The drug dealer immediately lunged for my throat.

"Get back, you asshole!" I braced my hands on his chest, struggling to push him away. His flannel shirt was wet with blood and as I fought with him, the fabric tore revealing a huge bite wound at the top of his shoulder.

Click. Click. Click.

The other two were almost on us. Panic had me trying to bring my knees up to kick him off.

He's too strong.

My arms shook with the effort of keeping his snapping teeth from my neck.

Just when my muscles began to fail, Brody was wrenched off me.

Gasping for breath, I watched in disbelief as the giant picked up the drug dealer and tossed him straight into Jess and the short guy.

They went down like bowling pins in a tangle of body parts and flailing limbs.

Before the giant could attack me, I searched the ground for my weapon. Finding my knife, I fisted it in my uninjured hand and swung it at the hulking creature.

In a blur of motion, he knocked the weapon away and threw me over his shoulder.

"Let me go! Help!" Blood rushed to my head as I beat my fists against his massive back.

The giant laughed as he carried me toward the parking lot. "Nathan didn't mention you'd be a handful." His deep voice rolled over me like thunder.

"Nathan Steele?" I asked feeling like I'd just been smacked with a lead pipe. *How does he know my ex?*

"The one and only," he replied. Answering my unspoken question he said, "Nathan told me, Gabriel, and Mason to bring you somewhere safe. If you hadn't noticed, the world is going to hell." He waved behind us where Jess and her friends still writhed in a heap.

I shivered, suddenly very willing to trust the stranger with my life. "Where are you taking me?"

The man twisted around to look at me with a surprisingly handsome face. In the light of the parking lot I made out the deep auburn color of his beard and hair. "Sanctuary."

"Where's that?"

Instead of answering, he made a beeline straight to a black SUV parked toward the front of the parking lot, opened the back door, and gently set me down on the leather seat. "I smell blood. Are you hurt?"

"I sliced my hand in the alley when I fell," I said, holding up my bleeding left palm.

He gently cupped it in his basketball-sized hand and frowned. "I'm sorry for scaring you back there." He lowered his head as if ashamed. "I seem to have that effect on females."

Although I didn't know him, he'd just saved my life and the last thing he needed to feel was bad about how I'd reacted to him. I reached out and touched his cheek with my free hand. "Thank you for what you did back there."

He turned his face into my hand and kissed my fingers. "Believe me, it was my pleasure. My name is Liam Murphy."

I sucked in a startled breath, taking in his beautiful deep green eyes. *Wow*. He's as sexy as the other two guys.

As if conjured by my thoughts, Mason and Gabriel came running out of the club.

Gabriel stalked over to the SUV and gave me a hard look. "You just needed to change, right?"

I dropped my hand away from Liam's face. "Um, well, I didn't know you guys were friends with Nathan."

"Give her a break," Liam said. "She just went toe-to-toe with infected in the alley."

Gabriel studied me. "Were you bitten or scratched?"

I shook my head.

Gabriel sniffed the air. "You're bleeding." He shot me an accusatory look.

I showed him my blood-covered hand. "I fell when I was trying to run from those..." I started to say zombies, but stopped myself. *They couldn't be zombies, right?* But what other explanation was there?

Mason peered around Gabriel's shoulder. "That cut needs to be disinfected. Let me get my medical bag." He walked around to the back of the SUV and opened the trunk.

Bag. "Oh no!" I glanced back at the alley. "I dropped my duffel bag in the alley." *Shit.* It held my phone and purse.

"I'll get it for you," Liam offered.

"Don't be ridiculous," Gabriel scoffed.

Those things are back there. I grabbed Liam's muscular arm. "He's right. It's not worth your life."

Liam's grin transformed his face from ruggedly attractive to drop-dead gorgeous. "I'd gladly risk my life for your happiness."

Gabriel's gaze narrowed. "Liam, forget it. Get into the car."

Ignoring him, Liam jogged back toward the alley.

"Damn it!" Gabriel slammed his hand on the roof of the SUV. "Happy now, princess?"

I sucked in a breath. "I didn't want him to go." *God, what if those monsters tear him apart?* My stomach knotted as I watched the alley.

A minute later, Liam reappeared with my bag. He carried it over and set it on my lap like a trophy. "Easy peasy."

Unable to help myself, I threw my arms around his beefy neck. "Thank you. Just don't do something crazy like that again."

He slowly pulled away, his deep green eyes never leaving my face. "I have a feeling that I'm going to be doing a lot of crazy things over you."

Heat moved low in my belly as I inhaled his scent—fresh pine with a hint of mint. I decided then and there that I liked Liam. A lot.

"For Christ's sake, let's get out of here," Gabriel snarled, opening the door to the front passenger seat and getting in.

We weren't just going to leave. *Were we?* "Wait. Shouldn't we call the police?" There were monsters in the alley, surely that warranted a call to the authorities.

"There's nothing they can do," Gabriel said tersely. "Besides they're probably overwhelmed with calls as it is."

I blinked at him in disbelief. "But we need to at least tell Max—"

"What we need to do is get to safety. Now, Liam," Gabriel growled.

Liam got into the driver's seat and started the vehicle while Mason slid into the seat next to mine.

"Step on it, brother. We've wasted too much time here already." Gabriel glared at me again.

As Liam pulled out onto the street, Mason tore open a package and the sharp, acrid smell of alcohol filled the inside of the car. "This may sting a bit." He gently pulled my injured hand into his lap.

That was an understatement. I hissed in pain when he started cleaning the cut.

Without even turning on a light, he reached for a spool of gauze and then expertly wrapped my hand.

"Are you a doctor?"

"I am." The flash of his even, white teeth made my heart pound a little faster.

Does he do backs? I wondered.

Liam caught my eye through the rearview mirror. "So what's the deal with you and Nathan? Are you two together?"

I shook my head. "No. I haven't spoken to him in ages."

"Really?" Liam said, flashing me another smile.

Damn. Liam was sexy in a mountain man kind of way. I licked my suddenly dry lips. "I was his daughter's nanny before we got together. We only dated for a few months before Nathan broke up with me." Realizing that I was rambling, I shut my mouth.

"He's a fool," Mason said softly.

"His loss, our gain," Liam rumbled from the front seat.

Gabriel snorted. "Eyes on the road, Liam. Nathan

wouldn't have us drop everything in the middle of the goddamn zombie apocalypse and go after this female if she wasn't important to him."

"The zombie apocalypse?" I repeated with a laugh. "You don't actually believe that, do you?"

All three men nodded in unison.

"That's insane."

"What did you think those creatures were in the alley?" Liam asked.

"I don't know...sick people," I answered weakly, trying not to remember how Jess's guts had hung outside her body.

Mason white-knuckled his medical bag. "They are sick. Sick and dead. And soon the entire world will be filled with them."

It suddenly seemed colder in the vehicle. "What are you talking about?"

Mason sighed. "The flu vaccine is causing pathogenic side effects in a sizable subset of the population. That older gentleman back in the club is a good example. He must've received the vaccine within the past twenty-four hours— that's usually how long it takes for the Z-virus to spread and kill a person. Like the other infected, he reanimated immediately after death."

I gasped. "Dr. Sullivan died?"

Mason put his hand over mine. "I'm sorry if he was a friend."

"He, ah, wasn't, but I didn't realize he was that bad off." *Crap, in less than an hour that guy went from drooling over me to dead.*

Gabriel cleared his throat. "The flu vaccine kills people and brings them back as zombies who infect and kill others."

"Holy shit." That explained the crazed people on TV and Jess's new undead look. As impossible as it sounded, I was starting to drink the Kool-Aid. "I have to warn my friends." I pulled out my cell phone and rang Sydney. My call went straight to voice mail. "Syd, call me as soon as you get this. There's some bad shit going on and you need to get somewhere safe." Hopefully, she was just finishing up with that bachelor party and I'd catch her before she got to the airport.

I tried the club, but the phone just rang and rang. *They must've already closed.* I then tried Donna's cell and then Max's. Neither one of them picked up. *Damn it.* I left Max a voice mail asking him to call me. He'd want to know about Jess and my dead VIP customer.

After ending the call, I stared down at the phone. There was only one more person I felt compelled to call. Even though I'd deleted his number from my phone, it was seared into my mind just like the memory of his mouth on my body. Taking a steadying breath, I dialed Nathan.

He picked up on the second ring. "Vana?"

The sound of his deep rumbling voice wrenched my heart. *How can he rattle me after all this time?* "Hi, Nathan," I managed to say through clenched teeth.

"Are you with Liam and Gabriel?"

"Yes, and Mason," I said with all the calmness I could muster.

"Good. They're going to take you to a property up in the mountains."

The mountains? "But that's hours away."

"The farther away from town you are, the safer you'll be. As soon as I get Mira, we'll join you."

"Where is she?" I asked, my throat tightening with worry.

"With her new nanny," he said in a clipped voice. "We'll see you shortly and then you and I will talk. I have a lot of things I need to tell you. I've missed you...I want you back."

A million different emotions flashed through me—confusion, pain, anger and a dump truck full of bitterness. "You're a few months too late for that."

"Vana." My name sounded like a plea on his lips. "I'm sorry. I can explain everything."

My breathing grew ragged. "Fuck you." Tears swam in my eyes as I thought of all those anguished nights I'd dreamed of him begging me to take him back. "You told me that I meant nothing to you and now you mean nothing to me."

"Vana, I—"

A loud crash sounded through the phone and our connection went dead.

ॐ *5* ॐ

LIAM

I'd never been a jealous man. In fact, I'd long come to terms with the fact that my size intimidated females, both human and Lykos alike. Other than the rare female or two whose curiosity temporarily overwhelmed their fear, they avoided me like the bogeyman I'd become. Over the years, I'd gotten used to seeing other males chosen by females. *So why did the sight of Doc's arm wrapped around Havana's slight shoulders make me want to rip the offending limb off and beat him with it?*

As if feeling my glare in the rearview mirror, Doc looked up. "Is something wrong, Liam?"

I enjoyed the scent of anxiety wafting off the smaller male. He might be better-looking, and a doctor, but we both know who was deadlier.

Gabe looked over at me. *"Why are you giving that poor male The Look, brother?"*

I feigned innocence. *"What look?"* The other Enforcers told me I wore a particular expression before going after someone who had the misfortune of pissing off Tasha. It was a running joke back among the rest of the Enforcers that

Liam's Look was enough to stop a male's heart from beating. If only. It'd make my work far less messy.

"Ease up or Mason will piss his pants," Gabe chided. *"That's an order."*

I swallowed back my growl. Gabe was one of the few who could speak to me like that without fearing for his life.

The dark-haired male gave me a puzzled look. *"What's going on with you?"*

I shrugged. Normally, I maintained an ironclad hold on my emotions. But seeing Doc plastered all over Havana set my teeth on edge. *"The female is pretty,"* I said trying to offer an explanation.

Gabe grunted in understanding.

My gaze shifted back to Havana. *Pretty.* That was an understatement. I'd never seen a more stunning female in my life and that included every Lykos female in our faction. But that wasn't very many if I was being honest. There were at least five males for every female, which meant that most males remained unclaimed like me. It was the female's choice after all and no female would ever choose a freak of nature like me. Having the reputation as the killer of killers probably didn't help my cause either.

But Havana didn't recoil in horror at the sight of me. Well, I guess she had, but later she'd touched my cheek. I couldn't remember the last time a female had touched me. The feel of her soft hand against my skin would fuel my fantasies for the next month.

Of course, now Doc was holding her hand. I glanced up in the rearview mirror and growled.

Doc flinched. *"What is it?"*

I scowled at him. *"She doesn't need you pawing at her."*

The smaller male let out an indignant sniff. *"I've never pawed at a female in my life."*

He probably hadn't needed to. Lucky bastard. No doubt

females threw themselves at the handsome male wherever he went. I gritted my teeth. *"Just give her some space."*

Doc dropped Havana's bandaged hand and shame pounded through me. She'd been injured on my watch. I should've protected her better.

Seeming to sense my darkening mood, Doc wisely moved to the other side of the seat.

The tightness in my chest eased. Unable to stop the impulse, I adjusted the mirror so I could better see the object of my obsession. There she was in a tangle of long dark hair. Her short black dress barely covered the tops of her tanned, toned thighs.

The sight of those long legs had me squirming in my seat.

Havana looked up and our gazes tangled in the mirror.

For a moment, I lost myself in her eyes. Back in the alley, I didn't notice their color, but now I could see they were a deep brown. *Beautiful.* Just like every inch of her. My heart pounded as I imagined her seeking comfort from me instead of Doc.

I'd put my arm around her and draw her against me. She'd sigh and pull me close and—

"Watch the road!" Gabe yelled, startling me back to reality.

I jerked the wheel to the left narrowly avoiding a car that had stopped in the middle of the street. "Sorry."

Gabe cursed. *"This was such a bad idea. I should've found a way to refuse Nathan. No way do we need to deal with a female like her right now. Look at you and Mason panting over her instead of focusing on our mission. She's the last goddamn thing we need."*

He was wrong. Havana was the only thing I needed. Fuck all those other females. Their fear and rejection no longer mattered. I'd been waiting for this female all my life and now she was here. I tightened my fingers around the steering wheel. *She's mine and no one, not even the doctor in the back seat, is going to get in my way. But... What if she doesn't want me?* Doubt crept in like shadows. *No female had ever chosen me—why will she be different?*

As if sensing my inner crisis, Havana said, "Thank you again for rescuing me back in the alley. I owe my life to you, Liam."

Her caramel-coated voice electrified every vein in my body. "I couldn't let any harm come to such a beautiful woman," I said proud of myself for delivering a line worthy of even the smooth doctor. "I apologize again for scaring you. My size can be intimidating."

Next to me, Gabriel snorted.

I fought the urge to punch him in the arm.

Havana smiled. "I find tall men incredibly sexy."

The curve of her blood-red lips made my heart beat wildly. *She likes me. Fuck. She likes me. What if she's the one? My mate.* I'd never heard of a human bonding with a Lykos before, but there was a first time for everything. I didn't share the same hatred the majority of our kind had for humans nor was I intimidated by the Council's law against interbreeding with them. The only reason I'd never approached a human woman before was because they seemed to eye me with the same fear Lykos females did. But Havana wasn't looking at me with fear in her gorgeous eyes.

I took a deep breath inhaling her heavenly scent. The sweet fragrance teased my senses and made my aching cock stand at attention. *Down boy*, I commanded, hoping that Gabe didn't look over and see the tent pitched in my pants.

A quick look told me I was the last thing on Gabe's mind.

The dark-haired male looked out the window, agitation rolling off him in waves. *"The majority of the human population was vaccinated yesterday or earlier today. Within twenty-four hours they will die, reanimate, and attack any living thing they encounter. Do you know what that means, Liam?"*

His words sucked the air out of the car. Immediately, my hard-on deflated. *"The world is fucked."*

"Pretty much. I hope Nathan knows what he's doing."

"Of course he does," I said automatically. The Alpha male always knew what he was doing. He was one of the smartest, strongest, and most courageous males in our faction. My trust in him was absolute and my appreciation to him for introducing us to Havana would endure for much longer than tonight. I thanked the powers that be that she was no longer his. An unclaimed female could choose any male. *Including me.* I grinned.

"At least one of us should've gone with him." Gabe drummed his fingers against the armrest of his seat so hard, his claws extended and dug into the leather.

I sent him a sharp look. Revealing ourselves in front of humans carried a death sentence. It wasn't like Gabe to be so careless. *"Brother?"*

He jerked up in his seat and fisted his hands. *"We should've forced him to come with us like Tasha ordered."*

I gave Gabe an incredulous look. Just because Tasha ruled the faction didn't mean we could force Nathan to do anything. Male Alphas were almost as powerful as their female counterparts. With one thought Nathan could force Gabe and me to fight each other to death. I shuddered at the idea of harming one of the few males I called friend. "He wanted to save his babe," I said softly.

"To what end? It's just a matter of time before Tasha goes after the child." Gabe let out a harsh breath no doubt reliving the horror of his past.

I grimaced. Our vicious ruler tolerated no other Alpha females in her territory. Not even her own offspring. It was common knowledge that the only reason Mira lived was because it gave Tasha leverage over the powerful Alpha male she still desired. *"That must be why Nathan wants us to go to Sanctuary instead of Winterhaven."*

Gabe let out a noncommittal noise. "Tasha will torture us if we return without Nathan." He rubbed his eye patch.

Tasha would probably torture us anyway. When bored there was nothing she liked better than to inflict pain on anyone around her. I dared voice the dangerous idea that had been worming its way into my mind. "What if we didn't go back?" Tasha would have her hands too full dealing with the chaos of the apocalypse to worry about two missing Enforcers. We could make a fresh start. One where I wasn't forced to brutalize and kill Tasha's enemies. One filled with a beautiful human female who didn't fear me. I glanced back at Havana who'd rested her forehead against the glass of the window. *What's she thinking about?*

Gabe gave me a sideways look. "And what would happen to your mother, brothers, and their children if Tasha found out you'd slipped her leash?"

The bitch will kill them all. I let out a heavy sigh. Even though they'd washed their hands of me a long time ago, I still cared for my family. "So what's the plan then?"

"We head to the lodge at Sanctuary. When Nathan meets us, we'll have to convince him to give his child to Havana." Seeing my sharp look he added, "She was the little girl's nanny. Anyway, then we bring him and Mason back to the settlement as ordered."

I laughed. "And how exactly are we going to convince an Alpha to give up his babe?"

"If he wants his child to survive, he'll see reason." Gabe took a deep breath and let it out. "It's the child's only hope. Tasha will never let her live—surely Nathan realizes that." The catch in his voice told me he was thinking about another babe. One that hadn't survived Tasha's ruthlessness.

"But how will the females survive on their own?" My chest

tightened as I glanced back at Havana. She was on the phone again. I wondered who she was calling.

"We'll find them somewhere safe to hole up, get them supplies, and hope like hell Tasha never finds them."

"Right," I said, a hollow feeling in my gut. I could only imagine what Tasha would do to Havana if she were to find her protecting Mira. The sheer fact the human woman had a romantic relationship with Nathan would be enough to earn her a painful death at Tasha's hand. *Or mine.* I flinched imagining Tasha ordering me to kill Havana. *I can't let that happen.* White-knuckling the steering wheel, I stopped at a light.

A commotion across the street caught my attention. Near the crosswalk, a mob of people surrounded a homeless-looking woman. She shouted at them and rammed them with her shopping cart. The largest male in the mob tackled her to the ground where the rest of them piled on top of her. Bile rose in my mouth. "Ah, hell."

Gabe turned on the radio to muffle the homeless woman's heart-wrenching screams. *"This town will fall by morning. We don't want to be here when it does."*

I glanced back to see if Havana had seen the grisly sight, but thankfully she was still on her phone.

Deciding that Havana's safety was my only priority, I slammed my foot on the accelerator and burned rubber until we got to the interstate.

6

HAVANA

We'd been traveling for at least three hours. First Liam cut south to the interstate, and then he took it north until we ended in bumper-to-bumper traffic. The past forty minutes, we'd barely crept forward an inch. It wasn't as if we could even pull off and wait it out at a rest stop. This far north of town there was nothing around us but open desert dotted by the occasional cactus and sagebrush.

I'd used the time to repeatedly call Sydney, Donna, and Max. No one had picked up. Filled with helpless frustration, I surfed the web reading horrifying story after story of people dying and coming back to life only to kill others. Feeling sick to my stomach, I left Sydney another message. "Syd, I hope you're okay. I'm headed up to Nathan's place in the mountains with some friends of his." I looked at the time. "Shit, by now you're probably at the airport. Please, please avoid anyone who has gotten the flu vaccine and if people start acting weird, get the hell away from them. I love you, girl. Call me as soon as you can." I ended the call with a sigh.

"You're worried about her?" Mason asked, studying me with his deep blue eyes.

"Yeah. Don't you have any family to worry about? A wife or girlfriend?" I tried to act like I wasn't fishing for info on his relationship status.

He smiled. "No. I haven't had time for romantic relationships in years."

"Oh," I said, happily surprised that the doctor was single. I could almost hear the ghost of my mom chortling in my mind. *He's quite a catch, Vana. Reel that fish in.* "What about parents? Siblings?"

A shadow crossed his face. "No. I...I'm estranged from my family."

I could tell it was a sensitive subject for him so I switched topics. "Did you grow up overseas?"

He chuckled. "Did my accent give me away?" In response to my weak smile, he said, "Yes, although I was born in the States, my adoptive parents raised me in England. I came back to locate my birth family," he paused, "and never left."

"Don't you miss home?" I'd never been out of the country. Hell, I'd never been out of Arizona, but England looked fascinating from what I'd seen in movies and books.

"Yes, I do." Mason sighed and ran a hand through his tousled blond hair.

"Winterhaven is his home now," Liam said, giving Mason a long look in the rearview mirror.

"Is it near Sunridge?" I asked naming the popular ski resort town in the mountains where I assumed we were heading.

Liam shook his head. "No. It's far north of the resort, deep in the San Angelo mountain range. It's pretty isolated."

"Never heard of it," I said apologetically.

"That's a good thing," Gabriel muttered.

"Is that where we're going?"

Gabriel twisted around in his seat. "No, we're headed to Sanctuary. It's a lodge about ten miles from Sunridge."

"Sanctuary. It sounds like a BDSM club name," I said with a weak laugh.

"You'd know," Gabriel sneered.

"Yeah, I would," I replied not about to let his cutting words bother me. I'd been on the receiving end of judgment for years. I was used to it. "What about your family? Assuming you weren't just abandoned on the street when your parents realized what an ass you were."

In the driver's seat, Liam stiffened.

A cold mask settled across Gabriel's face. "They're dead."

It was my turn to feel like a jerk. "Oh. Sorry. My parents are dead too. Well, my mom anyway. I never knew my dad." I clamped my mouth shut. *No one wants to hear your life story, Vana.*

"Is Syd your sister?" Mason asked in a gentle voice.

I shook my head. "No. I was an only child. Sydney's my best friend and roommate."

Mason gave me a reassuring smile. "I'm sure she'll hear your message and call you soon."

"I hope so," I said, looking down at the phone in my hand. Trying to keep the anxiety at bay, I said, "So how do you all know Nathan?"

The vibe in the car flipped as if I'd turned a switch. All three guys pressed their lips together and turned their attention to the surrounding cars. You'd think I'd asked them how much money they made in a year.

Liam broke the awkward silence. "We're all from Winterhaven and we work with Nathan occasionally. Well, at least Gabriel and I do."

"Oh." I let out a relieved breath. Given how weird they'd

acted, I almost expected them to admit to being ex-lovers. *They must work for the same company.* I didn't know much about Nathan's job other than it kept him incredibly busy and involved a lot of travel. That's why he'd hired me to care for Mira. He often needed an overnight nanny during his business trips. God, I hoped Mira was okay. I hadn't seen the little girl since the breakup. My throat closed up as I envisioned her scared and alone with those...things attacking her.

Mason made a soothing sound and brushed a lock of my hair from off my face. "You need to relax, Havana."

I rolled my eyes at him. *Right. Like that'll happen. The world was ending and I was just supposed to be all Zen about it.*

"What the fuck is the holdup?" Gabriel said, slamming his hand against the dash in a very un-Zen-like fashion. "We need to keep moving."

Liam opened his door, letting a cold rush of air into the vehicle. Seeming immune to the chill, he stepped out and peered at the line of cars ahead of us. As if he could see anything in the darkness. After a minute he slid back into his seat. "A semi overturned about a mile down the interstate."

My mouth dropped open. "You couldn't possibly have seen that. It's pitch-black out there."

"I have excellent night vision." He caught my eye through the rearview mirror. "And right now I'm really enjoying the view." He lowered his gaze to my legs.

I couldn't help laughing. The big guy was endearing as hell.

Gabriel looked at his watch again. "We can't waste time out here."

He needs a chill pill. "Why are you so worried about the time? Are you late for a date or something?"

He twisted around, his single dark eye pinning me to the seat. "Every hour we sit here, more infected are dying and reanimating. And trust me, princess, we don't want to be trapped on the interstate when the people around us start dying."

I swallowed hard.

Liam made a scoffing sound. "Ignore him. Gabe is always doom and gloom."

Gabriel glared at Liam. "Shut your hole, put the hazards on, and pull out onto the shoulder."

Liam batted his eyelashes at Gabriel. "I'm waiting for the magic word."

"Please," Gabriel ground out through clenched teeth.

"Now was that so hard?" Liam said, cranking the steering wheel.

It was clear through their interactions that the two men were friends. That was strange because they seemed like polar opposites. Despite his intimidating size, Liam was warm and friendly. Gabriel, on the other hand, could give snow frostbite.

Loose gravel crunched under the tires as Liam drove forward. We passed dozens of other cars, some honking at us in obvious irritation.

A few minutes later, Liam was forced to stop due to a Jeep blocking our path. Several dozen yards away, an overturned tractor-trailer was engulfed in flames. The semi must've been traveling north when the driver crashed into the concrete median blocking traffic from both directions. The orange glow from the smoldering fire illuminated two guys approaching the semi.

Gabriel cursed. "Fucking idiots. What do they think they're doing?"

As if answering his question, one of the guys, who looked like he hadn't seen the other side of seventeen yelled, "The driver is still alive."

Using a crowbar, the older guy, a potbellied man in a hunting cap, pried open the semi door.

Flames roared from the vehicle and a broad-shouldered woman stumbled from the truck. Fire covered her from her bald, blistered head to her charred cowboy boots. Impossibly, she lurched forward.

"Drop and roll," the fat guy shouted to her as he tried to beat the flames out with his jacket.

The truck driver snarled and tackled her would-be savior to the ground.

I felt the blood leave my face. "Oh hell!" *The truck driver is one of them.*

The fat guy screamed as he caught fire and the truck driver snapped her jaws around his throat.

Gabriel cursed. "No good deed goes unpunished."

The teenager stood in shock for a second and shouted, "Dad!" He rushed over in a futile attempt to pry the burning woman off his father. When that didn't work, he retrieved the crowbar and swung it at the woman's head.

The sickening crunch of metal against bone made me gasp.

Oh, God. I held my hand to my mouth as bile climbed the back of my throat.

The woman released the neck of the fat guy and rolled to her feet. Even with her skull partially crushed and fire consuming her body, she charged the teenager.

"Get back!" he screamed, swinging the crowbar like a bat. He backed up a step before realizing he was trapped between her and the burning semi.

In the distance, the fat guy stirred and slowly stumbled to his feet. Ignoring the fact that his shirtsleeve was ablaze, he gnashed his teeth and lurched over to where his son was barely holding off the advancing truck driver.

The people in the surrounding cars watched in shocked horror. None of them made any attempt to help.

"And so it begins," Gabriel announced in a dark voice.

"Someone needs to help the kid!" I cried, fumbling with my seat belt. I could at least distract the zombies so the teenager could get away.

"Mason, make sure she stays in her seat," Gabriel barked. "Liam, take care of it. Shoot them in the head, apparently body shots don't do shit." He shot Mason a withering look and gave Liam a handgun with a silencer attached.

I stared at him in shock. *What kind of guy carries a gun with a silencer?*

The kind you don't want to be stuck in a car with, my subconscious answered.

With a quick nod, Liam took the weapon and stepped out of the vehicle.

Mason rebuckled my seat belt. "There's nothing to worry about. This is what Liam does."

"What? Kill zombies?" I gasped.

Mason flashed me an enigmatic smile as we watched Liam step around the Jeep and fire two shots. The two burning figures collapsed to the ground unmoving. As the teenager stared at the smoldering corpses with a dazed look on his face, Liam shouted, "Is the Jeep yours?"

"My dad's," the teenager answered his voice cracking.

"I'm going to move it," Liam said, walking around toward the back of the Jeep. With a quick push, he shoved the vehicle out of our path. Then as if he hadn't just killed two people and moved a several-thousand-pound vehicle with his bare hands, Liam marched back to the SUV and slid into the driver's seat.

"Oh my God!" It was too much. People dying and coming back as zombies. Being in a car with a bunch of strange men who carried guns. I struggled to catch my breath.

Mason gathered me in his arms. "Shh. It's okay. The young man is unharmed. Just breathe." He smelled like rain. The fresh clean scent filled my senses, calming me with every breath.

I laid my face against his chest, feeling uncharacteristically drawn to him. Although I was usually the last person who trusted strangers, there was something about Mason that made me feel safe and protected. I definitely couldn't say the same for Gabriel.

The dark-haired man scowled over at me. "Happy now, princess. We stopped it this time, but you see what happens. All it takes is one infected. They attack and kill another person who reanimates and together they attack and kill more people. The entire world will be in anarchy by sunrise and within a week the majority of the population will be infected. The world you knew is gone."

Mason shot Gabriel a hard look. "Bloody hell, lighten up, mate. Can't you see she's hyperventilating?"

Gabriel sniffed and turned back around.

Numbness overtook me as Liam looked at me in the rearview mirror. In the dim light it looked like his eyes were glowing again.

My breathing grew choppier. *Is he even human?*

"Are you okay?" Liam asked, looking back at me with concern.

"She'll be fine," Mason said in a soothing voice. "Havana is a strong, courageous woman."

"You don't know anything about me," I said unable to stop my body from trembling.

"I know you were going to try to save that boy. That takes courage."

"Or stupidity," Gabriel muttered from the front seat. "Let's get moving."

Liam slowly drove us past the smoldering bodies and

wreckage. The traumatized expression on the teenage boy's face stayed with me. *Is this what the world is coming to?*

The sound of a siren rang out in the distance.

"Step on it," Gabriel ordered.

Liam hit the gas and we sped off into the night.

❦ 7 ❦

GABRIEL

The woman has to go. I twisted around to see that Havana had fallen asleep curled in Mason's arms. The doctor stroked her long dark hair with a look of naked possession on his face.

Next to me, Liam let out a low rumbling growl. My fellow Enforcer watched the rearview mirror more than the road. In all the years I'd known him, I'd never seen him react like this to a female.

She's dangerous.

The effect she had on these males was unprecedented. And they weren't alone.

Just breathing the air tinged with her exotic musk tightened areas low in my body that I'd been denying for years. The fact that my lust would awaken for this female defied reason. *Who was she?* I replayed the conversation I'd had with Nathan before we embarked on this mission.

Hours earlier, the Alpha male was just pulling out of his driveway when Liam, Mason, and I pulled up to his estate near the foothills. I'd jumped out of the SUV and jogged over to Nathan's expensive sports car.

The Alpha male rolled his window down and glared at me. "I'm on my way to a dinner party. What do you want?"

Most Lykos males would piss themselves when visited by two of the deadliest Enforcers in the territory. Not Nathan. Instead the male eyed me with a look of annoyance on his face.

"Tasha wants us to bring you home."

"This is my home," he said, baring his teeth in challenge.

I sighed. *This won't be easy. But then when is dealing with Alphas ever easy?* Thankfully, the strongest of us were rare as hell. Our faction only counted Tasha, her son, Tyberius, and Nathan among their ranks. Knowing that any more mention of Tasha was sure to meet with further resistance, I tried for another angle. "The Council has ordered all Lykos back to their factions."

Nathan's amber eyes widened. "Everyone?"

I nodded. "They believe the worst is coming."

"You mean—"

"Yes," I said, answering his unspoken question. "Liam and I just came from extracting Dr. Wheeler from the hospital. The entire place is swarming with infected. This town has twenty-four hours at most." Nathan couldn't be surprised at this news. For the past few days social media and television had played nonstop footage of hollow-eyed humans attacking and eating each other.

Nathan cursed and glanced at his Rolex. "I thought we'd have more time."

I shook my head. The entire human race was out of time. "If we don't get on the road now, there's a good chance we'll be trapped in Saguaro Valley." And although we were immune from the virus and could easily take out a few attacking infected, even the strongest Lykos would fall under a massive horde. At that thought, a chill crept through my jacket and swept down my spine.

Nathan ran a hand through his hair. Although the silver streaks in his dark hair had looked strange on him when we were boys, now it only added to his distinguished look. He reeked of money and prestige from his tailored suit to his perfectly manicured hands.

I, on the other hand, probably looked like a bum leaning on his expensive car with my black leather jacket and eye patch.

Stiffening, I reminded myself that I was the head Enforcer. Only the best fighters in the faction were hand-picked for the honor of being the Alpha female's personal guards. Although if I was being honest, indentured brute squad would probably be a better term for what we were. "Look, you need to come with us. The mountains are covered in ice. That vehicle won't make it to Winterhaven."

"We'll take the Rover," Nathan said, clicking a button on his dash. Behind us a door rolled up revealing six gleaming vehicles inside a vast garage.

I barely stopped myself from drooling over the sight of a cherry-red Porsche parked between a green Range Rover and a silver BMW. *Must be nice to be Alpha.* A bitter taste coated my tongue before I reminded myself that Nathan wasn't like Tasha. He'd never abused his power and had abdicated his seat on the Council in order to save his only child. That he'd gone toe-to-toe with Tasha and survived made him a hero in my book. *If he wants to drive himself, fine.*

"I'll ride with you." I started to telepathically relay the change in plans to Liam when Nathan said the words I'd been dreading.

"First, I have to go pick up Mira from her nanny's house."

Tensing, I said, "Tasha didn't lift Mira's banishment." How any mother could condemn her child to death was beyond my reckoning. I rubbed my eye patch as pain flared in my right eye socket. The constant throbbing ache was something I'd learned to manage except in moments when I was reminded of my greatest anguish.

Nathan froze, a fierce expression crossing his face. "That fucking bitch."

I couldn't agree more. But it didn't change one fact. "You can't bring Mira back to Winterhaven." If he did, Tasha would kill her immediately. Or even worse, force me to do it. My chest grew tight as I thought of my sister's child. *Isla never had a chance.*

"I know," Nathan said, rubbing his temples. "I'll take her to Sanctuary."

"The mountain lodge?" I asked unable to keep the incredulousness out of my voice. The luxurious vacation home had been built as Tasha's personal retreat.

Nathan nodded. "She'll be safe there."

In theory he was right. Although the forty-acre property and ten-bedroom lodge was impressive on its own, like all Tasha's homes, it was equipped with a below ground doomsday shelter. Only one problem. "Tasha will find out." This time of year, Tasha made frequent trips to the lodge.

Nathan growled. "I won't let that happen. Mira and Havana will be safe there."

"Who?"

"The female you're going to pick up for me tonight."

My mind swirled in confusion. "Who's Savannah?"

"Her name is Havana James, and she's a human that I want you and Liam to pick up on your way out of town."

"You want us to bring a human woman to Sanctuary?" I repeated slowly. My mind couldn't grasp that he would ask such a thing. The act of bringing a human to one of Tasha's homes would be nothing short of suicidal.

Nathan fished a phone from his pocket and tapped on it. "Yes, I'm texting you a photo of her along with the address to the club where she works. She's dancing there tonight."

"Dancing? As in stripping?" My voice rose several octaves. *Has the Alpha lost his mind?*

"Yes," he replied, his voice sharp as a blade. "She used to be Mira's nanny. She's special...very important to me." He looked up at me with an intense look in his eyes that spoke volumes. Clearly his relationship with this woman hadn't purely been a business one.

I shook my head. "I'm sorry. That's impossible. We have our orders." Alpha or no Alpha, what he was asking us to do would not only incur Tasha's wrath, but also violate every cardinal rule we lived by.

Nathan stepped out of the sports car with a lethal grace that had me backing up a step. Although on the shorter side for an Alpha, he was nearly eye level with me.

Refusing to meet his gaze, I stared at the setting sun behind him. It looked like the mountains were being dipped in fire.

"Look at me, Gabriel Perez," he said in a voice that rang with power.

Unable to fight his will, I glanced into Nathan's eyes. They glowed with the same golden hue as the sun. "You'll pick up Havana James, you'll bring her to Sanctuary, and you won't let any harm come to her. Do you understand?"

The compulsion in his words was so strong it reverberated in my skull like a gong. I gritted my teeth knowing it was futile to resist Nathan, just like it'd been futile to resist Tasha's horrific orders all those years ago. I bowed my head. "Yes, sir."

"Mason and Liam, swear to do the same," Nathan called out to the SUV in a voice filled with Alpha power.

"Yes, we swear, sir," the two males answered in unison.

Nathan bared his teeth in a facsimile of a smile. "Good. I'll pack and pick up Mira. We'll meet you at Sanctuary and then we can discuss the plan."

Just great. I'm sure whatever "the plan" is will get us all killed. Biting my lip, I nodded, stepped out of his way, and walked to the SUV.

Both Liam and Mason looked slightly dazed when I got back into the vehicle.

Liam rubbed the side of his head. "Fuck. Looks like we're picking up a female."

"Yeah," I said, grounding my molars together. *I can't believe Nathan used compulsion on us.* When Tasha found out he'd circumvented her orders, there'd be hell to pay. For him and for us.

Shaking his head, Liam followed my directions to the club. By his silence, I could tell he was livid. Of course, that was before he'd met Havana. Now he couldn't pry his eyes away from the female.

"Eyes on the motherfucking road," I reminded him for the twentieth time.

The big man punched my arm hard enough to leave a bruise and focused his attention back on the road.

With a heavy sigh, I glanced behind me and saw Mason tightening his arms around the woman.

Havana shifted in her sleep and her already sinfully short dress climbed farther up her thighs. I gritted my teeth and forced myself to look away. With a growing sense of dread, I realized she was no Atavus.

There could be only one explanation for why she was affecting me, Liam, and Mason this way. She was a latent Lykos who had yet to go through her transition. It was exceedingly rare for one of our kind to be found among the humans, but it happened. Hell, the doctor sitting behind me was evidence of that.

Once Havana went through her first transition, she'd instinctively seek out other Lykos. Or we'd hunt her down attracted by her scent. Havana couldn't be more than a week or two away from her transition. I could smell it in the intoxicating musk of her skin. I shuddered, my claws extending and retracting.

Just being around her fogged my mind with lust. *It's got to be the pheromones.*

When females transitioned for the first time, they entered their first heat. There was a reason they went into seclusion during that time. It drove every unrelated, unclaimed Lykos male in a ten-mile radius mad with lust. I would never forget the first time my sister transitioned and went into heat. My father and I had to guard her all night fighting off her would-be suitors.

Shit. Alpha order or not, there was no way we could bring this female back to Sanctuary. The three of us would tear each other apart to have her while we waited for Nathan to arrive.

I clenched my hands into fists imagining what would happen if the Alpha male found one of us screwing her. *He'd kill us slowly and painfully.*

Havana let out a soft noise in her sleep.

Liam looked up sharply as Mason made a soothing noise that settled her.

If we were to survive, I needed Havana as far away from them...and me as possible. *But how can I do that without bringing down Nathan's wrath?* I rubbed my jaw as I racked my brain for a solution. Outside, the sun peeked over the horizon illuminating the changing landscape. Desert shrubs gave way to large pine trees.

As we continued rising in altitude, I yawned, feeling the pop in my ears. At least we were heading in the direction of home. We'd be safe when we got there. Winterhaven was a sustainable settlement with all the food, water, and housing our faction would need for the foreseeable future. Due to her paranoia, Tasha had been forcing us to prepare for some cataclysmic event for years, and she'd make sure that, unlike the humans, we would survive it.

A wave of melancholy gripped me as we approached Sunridge. Even the remote ski town would be overrun by the infected soon. I studied a tight cluster of snow-covered cabins in the distance. The virus would rip through this place going from cabin to cabin.

Wait. Cabin. Yes. I grinned realizing there was a way I could fulfill Nathan's request without endangering Havana or taking her to the lodge with us.

I glanced over at Liam who was studying the sleeping female in the rearview mirror again. Neither he nor Mason would like my plan. *Tough shit.* I straightened my shoulders. As the head Enforcer I was in charge until Nathan returned and my word was law. *I'll make sure the female is no longer a threat to us all.*

8

HAVANA

"Wake up, love."

With a start, I opened my eyes and found Mason staring down at me. The sunlight streaming through the car windows backlit his blond hair, making it look like a halo. And his eyes. God, his eyes were as blue as the deepest end of the ocean. I wanted to gaze into them for hours.

"We're here," he said with a smile.

My face warmed as I realized I'd fallen asleep plastered across his chest. *What's going on with me?* I was never usually this comfortable with guys. Hell, it normally took me a couple of months of dating before I could even fall asleep next to a guy, and here I was drooling all over this stranger's shoulder after we'd met just a few hours ago.

Blinking away my fatigue, I looked out the window at snow-covered pine trees surrounding the SUV. *Snow!* I'd never seen the white stuff in real life. Excited, I sat up and a bolt of pain knifed into my spine. I let out a cry before I could help myself. *Damn it.* The pain pills had worn off. I cursed my last-minute decision to leave the bottle of oxy in my locker. Living with this constant pain was going to suck ass.

"What's wrong?" Mason asked his brows knitting together.

"Just my back," I said, giving him a strained smile.

"Let me take a look at it."

"It's nothing, just a recent injury," I said, waving my hand as if that would dismiss the throbbing pain. Noticing the empty driver's seat, I asked, "Where's Liam?"

"Getting your new home ready," Gabriel replied from the front seat. He pointed out the window at a small, dilapidated shack. The windows of the ancient-looking structure were boarded up, and the snow-covered roof looked ready to collapse at any moment.

What the...? "That's Sanctuary?" With a name like that I'd envisioned a fortified mansion or at the very least some kind of sturdy structure build in this century.

Gabriel let out a dry laugh. "Hardly. But it's where you will be staying for the foreseeable future."

Mason tensed next to me. "She should stay with us."

Gabriel glared at him. "It's not safe."

Mason jabbed his finger in the direction of the shack. "And she'll be safe in some cabin that's been abandoned for the past forty years?"

My heart pounded. "Wait, you're not really expecting me to stay in there, are you?"

Gabriel scowled at Mason. "It's not her safety I'm concerned about. She's a threat."

I gave him an incredulous look. "Says the guy with the gun."

Gabriel ignored me. "She can't be anywhere near us. Not if you want to live out the rest of your days."

"That's ridiculous," Mason said, wrapping his arm around me protectively. "She's not dangerous."

Gabriel cursed. "You can't even keep your fucking hands off her for a second and Liam's been mooning over her the entire drive. She's an attractive Ly—" He looked over at me and shut his mouth. After taking a deep breath, he said, "I've made my decision."

Mason tightened his arm around me. "You're wrong."

A tension grew between the two men so thick it made the hair on the back of my neck stand on end.

Gabriel bared his teeth. "Are you challenging me?"

Mason made a low rumbling sound in his throat. If the noise had come from a dog, I'd say it was a growl, but Mason was a man. *Right?*

Suddenly, the shack didn't look so bad. "I'll go look for Liam." I grabbed the handle and swung the car door open. The cold air burned my lungs and shook the last bit of lethargy from my limbs. Taking a deep breath, I stepped out into the snow remembering a second too late that my boot heel had snapped off. "Ah," I cried, barely stopping myself from falling.

"Havana!" Mason slid out of the seat and scooped me up in his arms. "Let me help you."

The abrupt motion sent waves of pain radiating down my back. Not wanting to ruin his chivalrous move, I bit back my moan of pain and let him carry me up the rickety steps of the shack. To think I'd gone my entire life without a man picking me up and in the space of twenty-four hours two mouthwatering men had.

Mason shifted me and opened the shack door with one hand. The door creaked so loudly I half expected the whole thing to fall off the frame.

I took one sniff of the dank musky cabin air and sneezed.

Mason laughed. "You sound like an adorable chipmunk when you do that."

"No, I don't," I said, playfully slapping his chest. I'd long been teased about my high-pitched sneezing.

Smiling down at me, Mason stepped across the threshold and his foot plowed straight through the floorboard. He fell forward, and I sailed out of his arms.

Moving so fast he was a blur, Liam snatched me out of the air. "Gotcha."

I couldn't stop the gasp of pain that escaped my lips when the auburn-haired giant gently set me on my feet. Wincing as I rubbed the small of my back, I said, "Wow, you move fast for a big guy."

"I've got all kinds of moves, beautiful," Liam replied with a wink. He looked over at Mason. "Sorry, I didn't have time to warn you. The floor is bad over there."

Mason tore his loafer free of the broken plank. "This place is an uninhabitable death trap."

I wholeheartedly agreed. The dark space was covered with spiderwebs and inches of dust. It contained only one room no bigger than the dressing room at the club. The only furnishings consisted of a small table and bench, a wooden rocking chair, and an old green-and-red plaid couch that looked like it might be home to a colony of fleas.

"Oh. It's not so bad. It's actually kind of nice with the creek right out back. Most important, the stove still works." Liam marched over to the large black woodstove in the center of the room. "I've cut enough wood for several days, just make sure to keep the stove going." He opened the rusted metal door to the stove to show me the fire flickering inside and then patted the four-foot-tall pile of logs he must've stacked next to the stove.

"She shouldn't stay here," Mason said, eyeing the small section of roof that had collapsed in the far corner of the room.

Liam straightened to his full height, the top of his head

skimming the exposed timber ceiling. "I agree, but it isn't up to me."

"It's up to me," Gabriel announced carrying in my duffel bag. He stepped over the hole Mason had made in the floor. As he set the bag down on top of the table, it sent a plume of dust into the air. Gabriel coughed, looking around the room. "Isn't this cozy? You know people pay a lot of money for rustic travel experiences these days. Who needs running water and electricity when you can have the sights and sounds of the forest?" He lifted his arms up and turned in a half circle. The heel of his boot crunched through another weak floorboard.

I'd stopped listening halfway through his monologue. "There's no running water or electricity?" Hysteria filled my voice. Roughing it was staying at a motel without cable. I'd never been camping before. I couldn't imagine anything more horrific than sleeping on the ground outside with nothing but a bag and a nylon tent separating me from the creatures in the wilderness. I glanced at the area by the door that probably served as a kitchen space. There was a rusted basin, but no faucets. "Where's the bathroom?"

Liam rubbed the back of his neck. "There's an outhouse out back, but I think a family of raccoons might be denning in there.

"Raccoons," I shrieked.

"No worries. We can bring you a bucket," Gabriel announced cheerfully.

"A bucket?" *This isn't happening.* I laughed. "Very funny. Joke's over. I know you aren't going to leave me in this dilapidated shack with no running water or electricity in the middle of the forest alone."

Liam and Mason flinched.

Gabriel pressed his lips together. "Count yourself lucky, princess. There's nothing around this cabin for miles. No houses. No stores. No people, which means no infected will find you and eat you."

"What about bears?" I cried.

"There are no bears around here. Your only threat is a couple of lonely wolves," Gabriel retorted.

I wrapped my arms around my chest. "Wolves?"

Mason shook his head. "Gabriel is making a bad joke. You're not in danger from anything. Liam stocked the shelves with some food we picked up from town. We'll bring more food and supplies when we come check on you. Won't we?" He gave Gabriel a hard look.

Gabriel returned his glare. "Come on, let's leave her to get settled in her new home." He strode to the door.

Desperate not to be left there, I played the only card I had. "Nathan wouldn't like you leaving me like this. He said you were bringing me to a safe place."

Gabriel whipped around. "This is a safe place, princess. Just because you're a pampered pet who's going to have to live without the finer things in life doesn't mean you aren't safe. Besides, given the way you spoke to Nathan on the phone, he probably doesn't give a damn about what happens to you now." He stalked through the door and marched out to the SUV.

Who the fuck does he think he is? I was no pampered pet. I'd been on my own since I was sixteen. Anger roared through me along with the desire to punch that ass in the jaw so hard he'd have to wire it shut.

"I'll be back as soon as I can," Mason announced.

I grabbed his arm, not wanting him to leave. "Please don't go." I despised the plea in my voice. There was only one thing I feared in life. That was being alone. Looking around, I amended that fear to being alone in a dark, abandoned cabin.

"I have to. For now." He gently twisted his arm free and kissed the top of my hand.

"Where are you staying?" I asked.

"The lodge is a few miles north of here."

"We aren't far and we'll be checking on you," Liam rumbled behind me.

I turned to see the big guy holding the head of a huge brown-and-beige snake in his hands.

I stumbled back a step. "What's that?"

He looked down at the serpent. "Nothing you need to worry about."

"You found that in here?" My voice climbed one note shy of shattering glass.

"It's more afraid of us than we are of him."

The creature shook its tail and a dry rattling sound filled the room.

"I highly doubt that," I squeaked. Trembling, all I could do was back away as he carried the vile thing to the door.

Liam stopped in the entryway and called back, "Remember keep the stove going, you don't want to lose your only heat source. There's supposed to be a big storm coming. It'll be cold as a witch's tit outside."

I nodded weakly. *This can't be happening.*

Mason headed for the door.

"Wait. Don't leave!" I begged.

An agonized look crossed his face. "I'll try to talk some sense into Gabriel. Hopefully, we can get you into the lodge in a couple of days."

"A couple of days? I can't stay here a couple of days." My throat constricted as I looked around the room in growing panic. *I can't stay here a couple of hours.*

"I'll be back," Mason promised. The door creaking shut behind him sounded like a coffin closing. My coffin.

"Oh, God." I swallowed hard and eyed the woodstove warily. "It's just for a few days." *Damn. I need to call Syd. She'll know how to survive in this place.* That crazy girl loved all this outdoorsy stuff as much as I hated it. She followed home-steading and canning blogs the way I followed fashion and celebrity posts. Careful to avoid the holes in the floor, I walked to my bag and pulled out my phone. *Of course there's no signal.* I sighed and carried the useless device to the couch. As I sat down, something moved inside the cushions.

I shot to my feet and an army of mango-sized rats poured from the fabric. Screaming, I bounded on top of the table. Hyperventilating, I watched the vermin skitter into half a dozen different holes in the walls. *Oh, God.* "I've changed my mind!" I screamed at the top of my lungs. "Take me back to town. I'll take my chances with the zombies!"

9

MASON

I glared at the back of Gabriel's head the entire five-mile drive up to Sanctuary. "We shouldn't leave Havana in that hellhole."

The dark-haired Enforcer didn't respond, but based on the angry looks Liam was hurling at him, Gabriel was likely getting an earful from his friend.

I could've tapped into their telepathic argument, but I saw no reason to tick both males off. Getting on the wrong side of Enforcers was never a bright idea.

I looked over at the empty seat beside me. Even though I'd known Havana for only a few hours, I missed her. She was a fascinating mix of vulnerability and sexy seductress. I'd never met a female like her.

Spying her discarded jacket on the floorboards, I bent down and picked it up. Unable to resist the impulse, I held it up to my face and inhaled deeply. Her amazing scent filled my nostrils making my stomach tighten with need. At once, my mind flooded with the memory of her incredibly soft skin and the rich, raven strands of her hair.

A growl escaped my lips. *I won't let her suffer in that hovel.*

She was an injured female trapped in that poor excuse for a shelter without a jacket or even proper footwear. Leaving her in that situation felt wrong on every level. Even if she hadn't been the most enchanting creature I'd ever met and her scent hadn't twisted me up inside, leaving any female to fend for herself went against both my human and Lykos instincts.

Neither Liam nor Gabriel should be okay with the situation either. A Lykos male's entire purpose was to care for and protect females, not endanger their lives. I opened my mouth to plead Havana's case again, but Gabriel jerked his head up.

"I don't want to hear another fucking word about her from either of you." He turned and glared at me with his one good eye. "We did our part. We got her out of town."

"But we were supposed to take her to Sanctuary." Liam pointed up the snowy road.

"Technically, the cabin is on the edge of Sanctuary land," Gabriel replied, crossing his arms. "She can't stay with us."

"Why the hell not?"

Gabriel snapped his head around to glare at me. "Because she belongs to Nathan."

I shook my head. "But she said they—"

Gabriel held up a hand cutting me off. "I don't care what she said. What I care about is what the Alpha will do if he discovers that one of you made a move on his female. He'll be here soon. *He'll* decide what to do with her."

I closed my mouth. I'd had enough interactions with Alphas to know that you didn't get between them and what they wanted. The memory of Tasha's face flashed into my mind. How naive I'd been when I'd encountered the ruthless Alpha female. Having lived among humans my entire life, I'd been confused and panicked by my first transition. My instincts had led me to Winterhaven where the sentries took me in and brought me to Tasha's chamber.

At the time, she'd seemed like a goddess with her golden hair and skin. *Little did I know she was a monster.*

After hearing the story of how I'd been found as a baby outside the Saguaro Valley Fire Department, adopted, and raised overseas, Tasha's citrine eyes had gleamed.

She'd stroked one of her hands over mine. "Pledge yourself to me, Mason Wheeler. Join our faction and together we'll track down your biological parents."

Dazed by her beauty and burning with the need to discover my origins, I'd readily agreed. Only later, when Gabriel had paid me a visit, did I learn the ramifications of my rash decision. The Enforcer explained that I now belonged to Tasha and she forbade any long-term relationships between humans and our kind. As such, any contact between my adoptive parents and myself would result in their immediate termination.

I'd been shredded when I realized what I'd done. Although my adoptive parents had always been rather reserved, I knew they loved me. No doubt they'd worried themselves sick over losing contact with me so abruptly, but there was nothing I could do to rectify that without putting their lives in jeopardy.

Months later, without delivering on her promise to help me find my birth family, Tasha forced me to accept a position at the Saguaro Valley General Hospital. Although I was an emergency room physician on paper, my true purpose was to screen the blood of patients for Lykos genetic markers. Tasha didn't want any others of our kind being lost among the humans.

There was no option of refusing the position. Gabriel had made it clear Tasha would torture me if I refused her request, and if I tried to run... Well the grim look on his face told me how that would turn out. By pledging myself to Tasha I'd lost my freedom and my family forever.

Even worse, just a few days into my new job, I was contacted by a private investigator. He'd told me my parents were searching for me. I had him relay the message that I'd located my biological family and no longer wished contact with my adoptive family. Telling those lies killed me, but it was the only way to keep them safe.

I hoped they were able to get to safety after the anonymous warning message I'd dared to send them about the coming epidemic. But I couldn't let myself be optimistic about their chances for survival. England was no better equipped to handle the masses of infected than this country. Unfortunately, most humans didn't have the foresight to build places like Winterhaven, or Sanctuary for that matter.

Outside the car window, the formidable eighteen-foot stone walls surrounding Sanctuary came into view. Ever suspicious of humans and paranoid of attacks by rival Lykos factions, Tasha had ensured that her vacation home, like Winterhaven, was one of the most secure locations in the region.

Liam stopped the car at the wrought-iron front gate, rolled down his window, and punched in a code on a keypad.

Immediately, the gate swung open revealing the driveway up to the massive timber-framed lodge. The eastern portion of the sprawling building looked to be under construction with tools, lumber, and heavy equipment lying under blankets of snow.

"The construction crews were recalled to Winterhaven yesterday," Liam said, answering my unspoken question. "They've been working night and day to finish the pool by the January deadline Tasha gave them."

"Pool?"

"Yeah," Liam said dryly. "Tasha wants an in-ground lap pool and sauna. And what Tasha wants—"

"She gets," Gabriel finished for him.

I shook my head. *Pool. Seriously?* As if the ten-bedroom luxurious mountain lodge equipped with a hidden lower level capable of withstanding a direct nuclear attack and outfitted with enough supplies to keep Tasha and her entourage going for years wasn't enough.

Liam parked the SUV by the front steps, and he and Gabriel got out of the vehicle.

With a sigh, I slid out of my seat and followed the two males up the impressive stone staircase.

As Liam tapped a code into another keypad by the door, he explained that a mixture of solar panels and wind turbines powered this property. Sanctuary would not be affected if and when the power grids went down.

The door clicked and Gabriel turned the handle and strode inside.

"What's the code?" I asked Liam as we stepped across the landing.

He ignored me.

I took a deep breath inhaling the scent of pine and lemon-scented wood polish. "Fine. I'll remember that if you ever need emergency medical care."

The giant grinned. "I like your grit, Doc. Few males have the balls to talk to me that way."

Under normal circumstances, I wouldn't either, but these were far from normal circumstances and I was tired of being ignored and pushed around.

"Since I sometimes work with the construction crew, I've been entrusted with the codes," Liam explained, shutting the door behind us. "If I were to give them to you and Tasha were to find out..."

He didn't need to finish the sentence. "Right." I made the mistake of glancing up at the massive antler chandelier hanging from the lofty wood beam ceiling. *Ugh!* This place reeked of Tasha's singular taste from the various bear pelts scattered over the gleaming wood floors to the countless animal trophies mounted over the stone fireplace in the foyer. My eyes bugged out at the sight of a taxidermied wolf captured mid-growl at the foot of the massive wood staircase. *Surely, it couldn't be...* "Is that one of ours?"

Liam glanced over at the wolf and gritted his teeth. "An unfortunate Lykos male from the Moon Valley faction. Tasha loves to display her kills. Fair warning you'll find them all over the lodge."

I shuddered. *Great.* "And why are we breaking into the psychopath's vacation home again?"

"We'll be fine as long as she doesn't find out." Gabriel said, staring into the wolf's glassy black eyes. "I'll touch base with Nathan and contact Winterhaven. Everyone working here should've been evacuated, but there could be stragglers. Liam, I want you to check out the property and make sure it's clear. The last thing we need is one of the cleaning staff or a construction worker discovering us here."

Liam grunted. "Tasha will expect us by nightfall. What are you going to tell her?"

"That Nathan and the coming storm delayed us. She'll buy it. She has to expect that the Alpha male will resist her orders." Gabriel looked over at me. "There's supposed to be an infirmary on the lower level."

"There is," Liam said, nodding.

"Good. Mason, go down there and do an inventory. Make sure you have everything you'll need."

"Need for what?" I asked puzzled.

"To continue your research on a cure for the Z-virus and save the world," Gabriel said, stalking off down the hall.

No pressure there. I turned to Liam. "Where is it?" Although I'd initially been consulted when Tasha wanted to add an infirmary to her fallout shelter, I'd never been on-site.

Liam motioned me to follow him down the hallway until we came to a library.

A low whistle escaped my lips as I glanced up at the massive collection of books. The pine bookcases stretched two stories tall and covered the length of the basketball court-sized room. Cathedral windows bathed the gleaming tomes in morning light. Despite my hatred for the female, I couldn't help being impressed. "I never figured Tasha for a reader."

Liam snorted. "She's not. She had this built for her son."

"Oh," I said softly thinking of the mysterious Alpha male. I hadn't had too many run-ins with Tyberius, but knowing he was also a book lover increased my regard for him.

Keeping my gaze locked on the books, I stepped around another taxidermied wolf. "This looks like a first edition," I murmured, reaching for a gold embossed volume of *Oliver Twist*.

Liam stopped at the next bookcase. He tugged on the spine of *Heart of Darkness* and the wall of books swung open revealing an elevator inside.

I laughed. "A hidden elevator behind a bookcase? It's a bit clichéd don't you think?"

Liam shrugged. "They don't ask me. Take the elevator down a floor. The infirmary is the second door on the right. You can't miss it. It's right next to the storage room."

I stepped into the elevator, but stopped the door before it closed. "You agree with me about Havana, right? There's plenty of space for her here." Hell, there was space enough for a quarter of our faction here.

Liam grimaced. "Yeah, but there is no budging Gabriel. When he's set his mind to something he can be one stubborn ass."

"Then you—"

Liam cut me off. "Don't worry about the female, Doc. I

plan on paying her a visit real soon." With a smirk the red-haired giant walked away.

"Asshole," I murmured from inside the steel box. As the elevator descended, I quickly stomped down my jealous reaction. *Havana wouldn't be interested in a brute like that.* She needed a male that would see to her care and happiness. *But how can I care for her when she's miles away?* Lost in thought, I stepped off the elevator and sucked in a lungful of stale recirculated air.

Recessed lights on motion sensors turned on as I navigated past what looked like a sleeping area. Across the underground passageway was a warehouse-sized space filled with aisles of canned and packaged food. *Not a bad place to ride out the apocalypse*, I thought as I strode through the next door.

The infirmary was just as I'd specified in the plans, with an exam table and two hospital beds in the middle of the room. Across from the counter was a wall of glass cabinets. Upon closer inspection, I found them filled with every kind of medication and medical equipment imaginable. If there was a life-threatening emergency, this room had nearly everything I needed to save lives. However, it also had virtually none of the specialized equipment and supplies I needed to continue my research on the Z-virus.

A soft electric hum led me to the back of the room where an upright medical refrigerator stood. I peered through the glass door and started at the sight of dozens of bags of blood stacked on the shelves. "Oh, yeah," I muttered remembering that Tasha had required her entourage donate blood in case they needed it in a medical emergency. *The bitch thought of everything.* I glowered, looking at the bags of blood printed with her name on them. She'd even donated several pints herself. As if the she-wolf would ever need a blood transfusion. Between her ability to regenerate any but the most severe injuries and the dozens of Enforcers who'd die before letting harm come to her, she was the last person who'd ever need medical attention.

Not like Havana. The cut on the beautiful female's hand could get infected and there was the issue with her lower back. I hadn't missed how she'd winced every time something jolted her. Since I couldn't continue my research, at least I could use my medical training to help her. I walked back over to the glass cabinets and rummaged through them until I found the supplies I needed. After a quick pit stop at the storage room, I marched back to the elevator. Gabriel and his orders could go to hell. I was a doctor and my job was to help those in need. *Right now Havana needs me.*

❧ 10 ❧

HAVANA

It took thirty minutes for my heart rate to return to normal. Then it took another thirty minutes of me kneeling on the table to rethink my choices from the night before. *I should've just gone to Max.* He and Justin would've thrown Mason and Gabriel out of the club, walked me to my car, and I'd be cozy in my rat-free apartment right now.

And zombies would be breaking down the door. I shook my head to dismiss that thought. *The authorities will get the vaccine reactions under control.* Running for the mountains was a complete overreaction and now I was stuck up here in this horrible place that didn't even have a bathroom. *Ugh. What kind of people choose to live like this? I'll bet the guys are staying somewhere with running water and electricity. Screw them!*

Would you? my subconscious asked.

Maybe, I answered honestly.

I flushed thinking of how amazing Mason's arms had felt around me. The gorgeous doctor was the whole package. Smart, handsome, and yet still considerate and tender. I could totally see myself falling for him. And Liam was tempting too.

The giant's ability to switch between fierce alpha male protector and romantic flirt was so freaking hot. The skank in me was dying to see him without his clothes. *I'll bet he's freaking huge.* My stomach tightened at the thought. *Damn.* Despite what I did for a living, I didn't normally lust after strange men. In fact, I hadn't gone near another guy since my breakup with Nathan.

Get a grip, Vana. They were Nathan's friends, and that made them off-limits. At least according to Gabriel. My mood darkened at the thought of the condescending one-eyed asshole. *What the hell is wrong with that guy?* It was clear he hated my guts and it couldn't just be because I tried to give him and Mason the slip at the club. *No.* There was something more to his coldness. Some woman had hurt him. Badly. I mentally gave that mystery woman a high five. He probably deserved it. *I can't believe he expects me to stay in this rat-infested shithole.*

I shuddered. How ironic to flee the zombie virus only to contract rabies and die.

The door behind me creaked open. Shrieking in surprise, I nearly toppled to the floor.

"Havana?" came a sexy accented voice. "Why are you crouched on the table?"

I spun around to see Mason standing in the doorway with a large box in his hands.

"There are rats everywhere!" I cried.

"Well, we can't have that, can we?" He dropped the box he was carrying and came over to the table. "Let me help you down."

Clutching his hand, I stepped down and stumbled on my stupid broken heel.

Mason caught me before I fell. "As amazing as you look in these boots, we have to get you better footwear."

"Yeah," I gasped through the flare of back pain.

He gave me a concerned look, his golden brows drawing together. "It's your back again, isn't it?"

"It's fine," I assured him as I stared into his hypnotizing blue eyes. *Have I ever seen another pair of blue eyes quite this sexy?*

"It's clearly not fine." His expression turned clinical. "Were you injured?"

After I told him about my initial fall and where the pain was on my lower back, he gently probed the area. "Hmm. It's challenging to diagnose conclusively without imaging, but I'd wager you herniated a disc."

I sucked in a breath. "That sounds serious. Do I need surgery?"

"Generally, no. In most cases, they heal on their own. What you need is rest and some pain relief." He pulled a bottle of pills from his pocket and handed them to me.

"Oxy?" I said a little too hopefully.

"No. Ibuprofen."

"Oh, well better than nothing." I opened the bottle and popped two pills in my mouth.

He held up his hand as if to stop me. "You should take those with—"

I dry swallowed the pills and set the bottle on the table.

He sighed and shook his head. "There's something else that might help." He walked over to the box he'd left by the door and retrieved a black, corset-looking thing.

"If you wanted me in lingerie all you had to do was ask." I winked.

His tanned face reddened. "It's a back brace that'll provide lumbar support and hopefully relieve some of your pain." He held it up as he walked back to my side. "It's Velcro and easy to put on. You'll want to wear it under your dress." He coughed. "I can wait outside while you change." He turned toward the door.

"No, wait," I said, stopping him. I didn't want to be alone

in this place even for a minute. Besides, the naughty stripper in me wanted to push this primal attraction to the doctor a little further. "Could you help me put it on?" I asked a little too breathlessly.

He grinned. "Well, I am good with my hands."

"Good." I reached behind me and unzipped the back of my dress.

I probably imagined the catch in his breath as the gown slid to the ground leaving me in just a tiny thong and the thin strip of fabric covering my breasts.

His eyes widened as they followed the curves of my body. "You're stunning," he murmured before clearing his throat.

The notion that he was as attracted to me as I was to him heated my blood "Should I take this off too?" I asked, pointing to my top.

"N-no. That's not necessary." His voice sounded hoarse. "Can you hold out your arms?"

I raised my arms.

He knelt down behind me and wrapped the fabric brace around the small of my back.

An electric current seemed to hit me each time his hands brushed my skin. I bit back a moan when his fingers grazed my hip.

"Does that hurt?" he asked.

I shook my head. *God, no. Quite the opposite.* I didn't know why I was getting so turned on, but just then I didn't care.

He grabbed my hips with his hands and gently turned me so I faced him. Then he adjusted the Velcro front of the brace. "That should work."

There was something undeniably erotic about having a gorgeous man on his knees in front of me. I whispered his name.

He looked up and moistened his lips. Lips that were inches away from my—

My stomach let out a growl so loud it disturbed the rats.

Mason jolted, looking between my stomach and the skittering noises in the wall. "Sounds like you're hungry."

Embarrassed, I nodded.

"Then let's get you something to eat." Mason helped pull up my dress and then all but carried me to the SUV parked out front.

I shivered as a cold gust of wind pelted us.

"Here's your jacket," he said after getting me settled in the back seat. "I'll get some heat going." He opened the driver's door and turned on the ignition.

I relaxed as warm air surrounded me.

He went back into the cabin and returned with a granola bar, dried fruit, and a box of cheese crackers. "Here's some food. It's not much. Sorry. I was trying to get back here as soon as I could."

"Looks great." My stomach rumbled in appreciation. It'd been nearly twelve hours since I'd eaten. I inhaled the granola bar and fruit, then tore into the box of crackers. Mason scooted in next to me and closed the car door. He smiled as he watched me eat. "I love a female with a good appetite."

My face warmed as I realized that I'd nearly finished half the box of crackers. *Really sexy, eating like a lumberjack, Vana.* I wiped crumbs off my chin with my hand. "You know I'm good here if you wanted to go battle the rodents of unusual size." I waved at the shack.

He chuckled. "As tempting as that sounds, would you mind if I sat with you a bit? I'm a little famished myself."

"Of course." I offered him the box of crackers and for the next hour we ate and talked. Mason was easy to chat with and I soon learned he'd spent his entire childhood and young adulthood at a private English boarding school.

"You must've been lonely," I said, wondering why his

parents had gone to the trouble of adopting him only to send him away.

He shrugged. "It wasn't so bad. At least I got to go home for the holidays."

"Yeah, the holidays." I winced at the memories of spending Christmases alone waiting for my mom to stumble home from the arms of whatever guy she'd been hooking up with at the time.

Mistaking the reason for my reaction, Mason looked at my hand. "Is the cut hurting?"

I shook my head. "No, it feels fine." Strangely enough, my entire hand was numb.

"Good." He leaned over and kissed the top of the bandage. "Just try to keep it clean and free from dirt."

"Like that'll be possible," I muttered, looking back at the shack.

Mason followed my gaze. "You won't have to stay there long. Nathan is on his way and I'm sure he'll insist you move to the lodge."

The mention of my ex sent me into a coughing fit.

Mason pulled a can of soda from his pocket and offered it to me. "You should drink something."

I waved it away. "Nathan doesn't care about me," I said when I could breathe again.

"You two really aren't together?"

"No, and after how he treated me, I wouldn't take the bastard back if he begged." My heart twisted at the memory of Nathan kissing Mira's mother in front of me.

The lines of tension around Mason's mouth relaxed. "I'm happy to hear that. Forgive my boldness, but I have to confess that I'm insanely attracted to you."

"Ditto," I smiled. A dark part of me wondered how Nathan would feel about me getting together with Mason?

Would it cut him to the bone the way seeing him with Mira's mother had destroyed me? Suddenly, I wanted to find out.

I locked gazes with the handsome doctor. "So what do you want to do about it?"

The sudden sexual tension that sprung between us stole my breath.

"I know we just met, but I want to be yours," he said in a husky voice. He leaned over, his lips inches from mine.

Damn. I knew in that moment that Mason wasn't a rebound guy or a one-night bed warmer. This was the love-you-forever-walk-down-the-aisle type of guy.

Am I ready for this? Unsure, I shifted away from him. "I could use that soda after all."

A fleeting expression of disappointment crossed his face as Mason handed me the can.

Refusing to meet his gaze, I popped the top and soda shot all over. "Ah!"

Mason cursed, opened the door, and tossed the bubbling can outside into the snow.

"I'm sorry," I cried, blinking away the brown liquid stinging my eyes.

"It's my fault. It must've gotten shaken on the drive over here."

I laughed at his chagrined expression. "Do you have a napkin or a towel or something?" I wiped my dripping chin.

"No, but..." He pulled off his jacket and offered it to me.

"I'm not using your jacket," I protested.

"Why not?" He swiped at the soda clinging to his lip.

Suddenly, all I could think about was how those lips would taste. Before I could stop myself, I leaned over and licked a sugary drop of soda off his bottom lip.

He inhaled sharply, his gaze darkening to a deep ocean blue. "Two can play at that." He leaned over and licked soda from my chin.

The sensation of his lips on my skin shocked me sense-less. All I could do was hold my breath as he continued to lick down the edge of my jaw.

Heat coiled deep in my belly. I clenched my thighs together as my core throbbed.

He paused. "Am I'm being too forward?"

"No, I have men lick drinks off me all the time," I lied.

He straightened and pushed the heavy curtain of my hair to the side. "You have soda here." He motioned to the base of my neck. He paused waiting for my permission.

Oh what the hell? It'd been forever since I'd felt attraction like this for anyone and I promised Syd that I'd give the next guy a chance. Arching my throat toward him, I said, "Then you better get to work."

With a groan he leaned over. The wash of his hot breath across my neck made my breathing hitch. Then with slow deliberation he licked and sucked the sticky soda from my neck.

"Oh, God." The feeling of his hot, wet mouth set my insides on fire. I threw back my head, feeling my nipples stiff-ening into hard nubs. Desire pulsed through me.

"Yes," I moaned when he followed the curve of my throat up to my ear and then down. Delicious shivers racked my body.

Groaning, he pulled me on top of him until I was all but straddling him on the seat. Then his lips found mine in a slow, sensuous kiss that made my head swim.

The kiss was different from Nathan's wild, carnal kisses. *Nathan...* Memories of how he'd kissed, touched, and owned me body and soul in the bedroom came flooding back.

With a cry I slid off Mason.

"What is it, love?" he asked, an expression of confusion on his handsome face.

"Nothing." I smoothed down the hem of my dress unwilling to explain that the ghost of my ex still haunted me.

"You know you can tell me—" He broke off with a curse. "Bloody hell. We have company."

I looked out through the window and saw a white truck headed down the hill.

Mason looked less than pleased. "It's Liam. Damn it."

Sucking in a shaky breath, I mentally thanked the giant for his timely interruption.

II

LIAM

The minute Doc took the elevator down to the infirmary, I marched straight out of the library. Having moonlighted with the Sanctuary construction crews whenever Tasha ran out of humans or Lykos for me to threaten, I had no problem finding my way around the lodge. I admired the craftsmanship of the furniture I passed. All my life I'd wanted to build things with my hands, not that I had many opportunities as an Enforcer.

As I passed the dining room, I caught sight of the fossilized stone dining room table. The massive slab of petrified redwood had been transported from California, delivered by a crane, and required nearly fifteen Lykos males to move into this room. *Females*, I thought with a snort. Their focus on aesthetics baffled me. *What did it matter if the Alpha female and her entourage ate off a regular old wood table?*

I'll bet Havana wouldn't care about something as frivolous as that. The dark-haired female's beautiful face flashed into my mind. She seemed the type who had her priorities straight. Her repeated phone calls to warn her friends and her desire to save that boy back on the interstate showed that she cared about the things that really mattered. I gave the oversize table one last glare and headed toward the chef's kitchen. *Even though Havana may not care about expensive tables, she deserves better than that filthy cabin.* I cursed Gabe's stubbornness as I headed to the walk-in pantry.

Thanks to Tasha's mandate that the lodge be kept ready for her at all times during the winter months, the kitchen was fully stocked. I quickly loaded up a crate of food to take to Havana and added some pots, pans, and other kitchen supplies she'd need.

I didn't understand why Gabe wouldn't bring the beautiful female to the lodge. He'd been compelled by Nathan to keep Havana safe and there was no doubt she'd be safest here with us. But it'd be a waste of time arguing with him. From years of experience, I knew there was no swaying Gabe when he'd made up his mind.

After setting the crate by the door, I found some cleaning supplies and an unused water cooler sitting next to a five-gallon jug of water. I quickly added them to the pile. Then I jogged upstairs and walked into the closest bedroom. It was lavishly decorated, like all the rooms in the lodge, and I had to tear at least a dozen throw pillows off the oversize king bed in order to strip off the plush brown comforter. I was tempted to leave the decorative pillows, but then figured Havana might like them too. Bundling them inside the comforter, I headed back downstairs.

As I set the bedding near the crate, I realized Havana didn't have a bed to put the pillows or the comforter on. I backtracked upstairs and searched the rooms until I found a smaller mattress and box spring. I brought them downstairs and then added a rug and leather recliner I'd found in one of the rooms. *She'll love the cabin by the time I get through with it,* I thought with a burst of satisfaction.

Since there was no way I was getting all the furniture into

the back of the SUV, I went in search of another vehicle. Thankfully, I quickly found a work truck one of the construction crew members must've left behind. The truck bed was half-filled with tools and lumber, but that was a good thing given the extensive work the cabin needed.

Filled with eagerness to see the lovely female again, I nearly ran Gabe over as I pulled the truck up to the front steps of the lodge.

The head Enforcer's face was contorted in rage and his breath fogged the chilly air. "What do you think you're you doing?"

"What does it look like?" I replied, stalking by him.

He followed me up the stairs and into the hallway that was barely maneuverable due to all the supplies and furniture I'd stacked in it. "What's all this?"

I hefted up the mattress and box spring. "Just a few things I'm bringing to the cabin."

"You're not going there," he said, trying to block my way back to the truck.

He may be in charge, but I'm off the clock. "Move." I sideswiped him with the mattress.

He steadied himself and glared at me. "You can't have Havana. She belongs to Nathan."

"She doesn't seem to think so," I said, loading in the bed. "But if it makes you breathe easier, I'm just bringing over a few things to make her more comfortable. I'll drop this stuff off and come straight back here."

"Right," Gabe said, watching me load up the rest of the stuff with a dark expression on his face. "You realize Tasha will have your balls when she finds her things missing."

"Fuck Tasha," I said under my breath.

Gabe rushed at me so fast he was a blur. He grabbed me by my collar and dragged my face down toward his. The deadly expression in his one dark eye froze my blood. "Perhaps you need a reminder of the kind of punishment the Alphas can dole out," he growled. He sent flashes of his memories to me.

Agonized screams rang in my mind. I shuddered at the images of Lykos losing their lives. Males. Females. A newborn babe. I clamped my eyes shut as Gabe's anguish slammed into me like a tidal wave. *How could he survive such loss?*

"Unlike you, I have no trouble remembering what she's capable of." Gabe flipped up his eye patch showing me the yellow diamond Tasha had placed in the socket of his right eye. Since the stone prevented the male from regenerating the organ she'd torn out of his head, and she'd compelled him never to remove it, he was left in a constant state of agony.

I sucked in a breath. I'd never quite comprehended the depths of Gabe's pain until now. I clamped my friend on the shoulder. "I'm sorry, brother. I'll be sure to bring everything back. Tasha will never know."

Gabe flipped his eye patch down. "Let's hope not. I've been in contact with Winterhaven and informed them that we are going to be delayed by the storm. Tasha will be expecting us as soon as it clears."

My mood sank at the thought of returning to Winterhaven. I glanced up at the gathering storm clouds. "I'd better get this stuff delivered before the worst of it hits."

"Be quick and make sure Mason returns with you." Gabe nodded at the empty spot where the SUV had been parked.

That motherfucker took my car! I couldn't believe I'd been too distracted to notice. There was no doubt in my mind where he'd gone. *Damn it. Doc better not be putting the moves on Havana.* I fisted my hands. "Yeah, I'll be sure to bring Doc back with me." *Alive or dead.* Muttering curses under my breath, I jumped into the truck and hauled ass through the snow.

I wasn't about to lose this beautiful female to the smaller

male. Doc wouldn't be able to protect her like I could and Havana needed a male who could keep her safe. Especially now with the world in chaos.

You can't have Havana. She belongs to Nathan. Gabe's words rang in my mind.

I punched the steering wheel. *I don't care.* I'd never wanted a female the way I wanted her. In fact, I'd be willing to forsake my family and take on Nathan if Havana would have me.

All my life I'd been passed over by one female after another. Not one had ever looked at me like Havana did. Even my own mother had referred to me as "that freak." She'd seemed happy that Tasha had picked me out of the schoolyard to join the Enforcers. Better me lose my childhood and freedom than any of my precious older brothers. Mother had great hopes for them. Unlike me, they'd all been chosen by females and had given her the grandchildren she craved. At first, I too had loved seeing my nieces and nephews. Then they began trembling in fear when I'd visit. Feeling even more unwelcome in my family's presence, I'd stopped dropping by. Not that any of them had cared.

As the cabin came into view, my chest tightened. *Maybe Havana can grow to care for me?* That thought filled me with something I hadn't had in a long time. Hope.

That hope faded as I parked the truck next to my SUV and spied Doc straightening his clothes through the vehicle window. *Damn it, I'm too late.* Jealousy and rage clawed at me. For a moment, my inner wolf threatened to emerge. I took a deep breath and slowly let it out.

Doc shot me an annoyed look as he opened the back door and jumped out. "What's all this?" he asked, motioning at the overflowing bed of the truck.

It took all my self-control not to bound over there and rip his head off his body. Swallowing my anger, I stepped out of the truck. "A few things to make the cabin nicer for Havana."

The lovely female slid out of the SUV behind Doc and held the edge of the door with her bandaged hand as if for balance.

It was impossible, but she looked even more beautiful than she had just a mere hour ago. I took a deep breath, inhaling her intoxicating scent. My body's reaction to it was instantaneous. "Hello, beautiful."

"Hi, Liam." Her cheeks were flushed and her gaze hungry as she gave me a once-over.

Clearly the decision to ditch my jacket and sweater was a good call. It looked as if the female liked the tight short-sleeve T-shirt I was wearing. Unable to help myself, I flexed a bicep.

She licked her lips, her eyes glued to my muscles.

Take that Mr. MD.

Doc looked between us with an annoyed expression on his face.

I grinned. *Not all is lost after all.* Schooling my face into a grimace, I stalked over to Doc. "You were instructed to stay in the lodge."

To his credit, the smaller male met my glare unflinchingly. "Havana needed help."

"Help, huh?" I leaned down and sniffed the sweet scent of the female clinging to his jacket. "You kissed her." Based on Havana's blush, I knew I'd guessed correctly.

Doc's blue eyes narrowed in challenge. "Yes, I did."

"But that's all you did," I guessed based on the coiled tension in the smaller male's body and the fact that Havana was still clothed. "And that's all you're going to do." *If I have anything to say about it.*

"*She wants me,*" Doc growled into my mind.

I couldn't help taunting him. *"Only because I wasn't here. Don't you see the way she looks at me?"*

Doc scowled. *"She's just never seen a living behemoth before. Don't mistake awe for attraction."*

Realizing that Havana was watching our silent exchange with a look of confusion on her face, I disguised my anger with a smile. "Sounds like you're jealous, Doc."

The male gritted his teeth.

Dismissing him, I walked over to Havana. "Let me help you back into the cabin, beautiful. We'll get the place cleaned up and then I'll show you how a real male kisses."

Her shocked laugher filled me with happiness as I gently swooped her into my arms and carried her back inside.

HAVANA

Two and a half hours later I was seriously reconsidering my position on the shack. Liam and Mason had worked tirelessly scrubbing every inch of the place until not a spec of dust or a cobweb was visible.

Despite my many attempts to help, neither man allowed me to lift a finger. After cleaning the rocking chair and setting it by the woodstove, both men insisted I sit in it while they worked. And boy did they ever work.

Liam, proving to be quite the handyman, had repaired the holes in the roof and in the floor and best of all he'd covered all the cracks in the walls where the rodents had fled.

After assuring me they were mice, not rats, as if that made any difference, Liam applied a peppermint-smelling liquid along the floorboards that he said would repel any pests. I wasn't sure what rats, snakes, and bugs had against the Christmassy scent, but I resolved to douse myself in peppermint from now on.

Mason worked on creating a makeshift bathroom by hanging a thick wool blanket around the far corner of the room. He situated a bedpan and some toilet paper inside the space. I wasn't thrilled with the setup, but it sure beat trudging through the snow to fight the raccoons for the outhouse.

At my insistence the two men had carried out that nasty couch and replaced it with the furnishings Liam had packed into the truck.

I'd squealed like a little girl when they rolled out an enormous white cashmere area rug that must've cost a fortune. I had to kick off my boots and wiggle my toes through the soft fibers. Then they brought in a large leather recliner and a full-size bed complete with box spring, deep chocolate-colored bedding, and armfuls of matching decorative pillows.

"Bloody hell. What's up with all the pillows?" Mason asked Liam as they finished setting up the bed.

"Females love pillows. Don't they?" Liam looked over at me for confirmation.

"Of course," I replied, not wanting to hurt the giant's feelings.

He grinned and set up the water cooler he'd brought me.

Mason sat down on the bed as if testing its weight. "You should've grabbed a king, mate."

"I thought about it." Liam lifted the five-gallon bottle of water onto the cooler. "But it wouldn't fit in here."

"I guess we'll have to make do." Mason winked at me.

I couldn't help laughing at his surprising boldness.

Liam straightened and gave Mason a dark look. "The only thing you'll be making is a drink for Havana." He turned to look at me. "What would you like? I've brought instant coffee, some cocoa—"

Mason snorted, interrupting him. "I'll bet she'd like a nice cup of hot tea. Tell me you packed tea?"

Liam nodded. "And a teakettle."

"Excellent." Mason beamed and looked over at me. "You like tea, don't you?"

Although a cup of coffee sounded better, I nodded. "Tea sounds perfect."

Liam reached into the crate he'd set by the table, retrieved a teakettle, and chucked it at Mason's head.

Mason caught the silver kettle in midair. "Hey, don't be a sore loser."

"I've lost nothing," Liam said, shoving the recliner next to my rocking chair. He sat down next to me. "Are you liking the place better?"

I nodded. Despite my early reservations, I couldn't deny the spruced-up place had charm.

Liam had pried the boards off the large picture windows and the view overlooking the snow-covered pine trees and ice-crusted creek behind the cabin was breathtaking. I could almost see where someone would want to visit a place like this. *Almost*.

"Good," Liam said, reaching over and squeezing my uninjured hand.

Mason glared at us.

Not wanting to add to the crackling tension between the men, I tugged my hand free.

Giving Liam a triumphant look, Mason filled up the kettle with water from the cooler and set it on the flat top of the woodstove.

"You can cook on that thing?" I asked, curious.

"Of course," both men replied in unison.

Feeling like an idiot, I watched Mason put another log into the stove.

Liam pointed over at the crate. "I've brought you cookware along with some canned soups, chili, and oatmeal. Between that and the food I'll be bringing you, you won't starve."

"You'll visit me again?" I was already dreading the moment when both men would leave.

Liam grinned. "You couldn't keep me away if you tried."

Mason walked over to the crate and frowned. "There's no tea in here."

Liam twisted around in the recliner to look at him. "It must've fallen out in the truck. The doors are open if you want to check."

Mason walked to the door. "I'll be right back."

"Take your time," yelled Liam.

As the door closed, I reached over and grabbed the giant's hand. "I really appreciate what you did to this place."

He laid his other hand over mine. "Enough to give me a thank-you kiss?" He puckered his lips.

"If that's what you'd like in payment," I flirted back. I stood and leaned over him planning to kiss him on his cheek.

His playful expression transformed into an intense one. Before I could react, he hauled me into his lap and kissed me full on the mouth. At my gasp, he deepened the kiss. His lips were soft as velvet and his minty taste heated my blood.

My senses imprinted with the scent of him, pine, mint, and raw male. Arousal flooded my body as my heart took up the same wild beat as his.

He conquered my mouth with darting strokes of his tongue while his hands stroked me from hip to breast along the outside of my dress.

"Oh my!" I moaned when we broke for air. The fire that Mason had stoked in the car flared back to life. Sweet need burned through me. *What's happening?*

Nathan had been the only man I'd ever wanted this badly. Now in the space of a few hours I was losing my mind over two almost-strangers. *Go with it,* the hot needy part of me urged.

I shifted over Liam, my knees embedding in the leather armrests of the recliner.

He groaned as I rocked against the impossibly huge erec-tion straining the fly of his jeans.

I licked my lips, wanting more than anything to see what kind of heat he was packing. I stroked my hand over his fly eliciting a husky moan from his lips.

Mason cleared his throat behind us. "I step out for one bloody minute..."

A wave of shame and embarrassment rushed through me. *Crap.* How could I have forgotten he was here? *Not cool, Vana.* I had my slutty moments, but this was a new low even for me.

Liam grabbed my hips possessively. "I was just claiming my thank-you kiss."

"It looked like you were doing more than that," Mason said, his voice deepening. "Release her." He fisted his hands, crushing the box of tea he was holding.

Liam stiffened. "Or you'll do what?" His green eyes blazed with an unearthly glow.

In a split second, the giant had gone from sexy hunk to frightening beast.

Mason, who seemed to have grown several inches, let out a hair-raising growl.

I trembled, looking between the two men in alarm. They looked seconds from attacking each other and no part of me wanted to see these men beat themselves bloody over me. There was only one way to diffuse the situation. A thrill rushed through me at the forbidden idea. Summoning my stripper persona, I said, "Boys, don't get yourselves worked up. There's more than enough of me to go around."

Both men blinked at me in confusion.

I tossed my hair back. "Mason, why don't you come over here and join us?"

Liam tensed beneath me. "You want both of us?"

"Why not? Double the pleasure." I crooked my finger at Mason. "Are you game?"

Mason stood frozen for a minute. The fierce expression on his face faded as he exchanged a long look with Liam.

After a moment, both men nodded as if they'd just carried on a silent conversation and come to an agreement.

Mason set the box of tea down on the table and slowly walked over. A myriad of expressions flitted across his face including jealousy, curiosity, and scorching lust. When he reached me he pulled me up into a kneeling position over Liam. Then he kissed me, his lips firm and possessive.

Desire sizzled through me as I arched up into Mason's passionate assault. Mounting excitement blocked my twinge of back pain.

The sweet flavor of his lips exploded on my tongue, so different from Liam's minty taste.

Liam cupped my ass. "You're a kinky one, huh?"

"You don't even know the half of it," I murmured against Mason's lips. The things Nathan introduced me to… *Nathan*. I stiffened at the thought of him. *Fuck him. Let him stew when he finds out I got with not one but two of his friends.* With that thought, I swept aside my memories of him.

Mason let out another one of those sexy growls and stepped behind me. He moved my hair to the side and planted a kiss at the back of my neck.

I shivered as an electric current zipped straight from his lips to my aching core.

Liam's hands slipped under my dress and kneaded my ass. "I've never been with a female before."

That blew my mind. I hid my shock by leaning over and kissing his lips. "There's a first time for everything, big guy."

"I've never shared a female before," Mason murmured into the shell of my ear.

"Well, you're in for a treat," I said way too confidently. I'd been with two men at the same time only once before and only because of Nathan. My breathing hitched as I once against tried to banish the memory of my ex. *No. I won't let him ruin this.*

Mason found the zipper of my dress and dragged it down.

The warm air caressed my skin as the black fabric gaped open in the back.

Mason pushed the straps of the dress off my arms. The top of the gown pooled at my waist leaving only my dance top to shield my breasts.

"Take it off," I ordered in my sultry Mistress Robin voice.

With deft fingers, Mason removed the back brace. Then he undid the straps to my silver-studded top and bared me to their gazes.

Both men inhaled sharply.

"Fuck, you've got gorgeous tits," Liam groaned.

I laughed, not at all minding their obvious fascination.

With his arms wrapped around me from behind, Mason cupped my breasts. "I agree. These are exquisite like every inch of your body." He rolled a nipple between his thumb and forefinger eliciting a moan from my lips. Then he applied a delicious amount of pressure to the swollen peak.

The shocking pleasure-pain sensation shot me straight into a memory of Nathan clamping my nipples. *Take it for me, honey. It'll hurt so good.*

The memory was so real I could almost smell Nathan's sandalwood cologne in the air. "Ah." With a cry I pushed Mason's hands away.

He jerked back in surprise.

Liam blinked. "Is something wrong?"

Tears welled in my eyes. "I'm sorry. I-I'm having a difficult time getting over my last relationship."

"I see," Mason said slowly, moving over to the side of the recliner.

Liam's eyes widened in understanding. "You still love Nathan."

I shook my head. "No. I hate him, in fact. He made me fall for him and then he hurt me in a way no one ever had before. Now it's hard for me to..."

"To let yourself get close to someone again," Mason finished for me.

"Yes," I whispered, trying to ignore how my body throbbed with raging desire.

Liam thumped his chest. "I'd sooner cut my heart out than hurt you."

"I feel the same," said Mason. "I hope in time we can help you rebuild your trust in males." He looked over at Liam. "We should go."

My body howled in protest. "Please don't leave. I want to try again." I needed to try again. *This time I won't think of the bastard.*

Mason searched my face. "Are you certain, love?"

I nodded, never more sure of anything in my life.

"Okay, but tell us the moment you want to stop."

I threw him a wicked smile. "I don't ever want to stop." There were a couple of just-in-case condoms in my duffel bag from back in the day. We were set. *Let's do this.* Licking my lips, I pressed my breasts against Liam's lips.

The big guy's eyes lit up as he took one of my nipples into his mouth.

I moaned at the delicious sensation of his lips on my sensitive peak.

Mason let out a frustrated sound.

I gave him an arch look. "Didn't you say you were good with your hands?"

He flashed me a masculine smile, took his previous position behind me, and slid his hands down to my thighs. He swatted Liam's hands. "Out of the way, mate."

Liam shifted his hands to the small of my back, never

taking his lips from my nipple. The rasp of his beard against my skin made me shiver.

"This will feel so good, love," Mason whispered.

I gasped as he slid his fingers beneath my thong and caressed my damp flesh.

"Do you like that?" he rasped against my ear.

All I could do was whimper as he found my swollen bud.

Mason stroked me slowly at first and then faster.

Pleasure streaked through me. I grabbed Liam's shoulders to steady myself. My knees quaked, threatening to give out.

Mason pressed me back against his chest. I could feel his arousal pressing into my back. The fact that I was pinned between two men who wanted me stoked my desire even higher.

While continuing to work my clit with his right hand, Mason slid two fingers of his left hand into me and found my G-spot.

I cried out.

On the stove, the teakettle whistled and shook.

"Oh, God!" It was too much. The delicious pressure at my core combined with the erotic pull of Liam's mouth on my nipples sent me spiraling into a mind-blowing climax. Screaming, I shattered and collapsed boneless over Liam's chest.

The sound of our ragged breathing cut through the shrieking kettle.

"I'll get that," Mason said, pulling away and moving the kettle from the woodstove.

I pushed myself off Liam's lap on shaking legs. As soon as I stood, my unzipped dress pooled to the floor.

Both men gasped.

This is only the beginning I realized with a smile. *They're mine. All mine.*

With their gazes following every movement I made, I

sauntered over to the bed and sat down. Using my Mistress Robin voice, I said, "Take off your clothes and come over here." I patted the top of the mattress.

Liam leaped from the chair and whipped off his shirt.

The sight of his muscular chest took my breath away. *Wow. Just wow.*

Mason pulled off his jacket and polo revealing lean tanned muscles that made my mouth water.

There was something predatory in the way the men stalked toward the bed. They loomed over me, their bodies tense and hard.

Heat suffused me, filling me with such need, I whimpered. *How will we do this? Who will go first? Or will we all be together at the same time?* Overcome with desire, I watched the men approach.

Suddenly, the door crashed open and Gabe rushed in wearing nothing but his eye patch.

❧ 13 ❧

GABRIEL

The sight of Havana sprawled out nearly naked on the bed, with Liam and Mason standing over her sucked all the air out of my lungs. For a moment, my anger was replaced by a lust so fierce it turned my shaft to granite. The entire cabin was filled with the powerful musk of her desire. Each inhale of her scent eroded my self-control.

I couldn't rip my gaze away from Havana. Her beautiful breasts were more than a handful and those dusky nipples were begging for my touch. Her smooth skin looked like it'd been dipped in honey and a tiny scrap of fabric covered her cleft. A growl escaped my throat as I battled the urge to tear off her panties and bury my face between her legs. *She'll taste amazing.* I licked my lips and took one step forward.

Havana blinked up at me from the bed. "Looks like you want to join in on the action. The more the merrier." She patted the mattress next to her.

Immediately realizing I wasn't there for fun, Liam stepped protectively in front of her. "Gabe, I can explain."

Mason threw a comforter over Havana. "Before you get

upset, mate, you should know we're all consenting adults here."

Their words slapped some sense into me. I took a deep breath through my mouth knowing I couldn't afford to scent any more of Havana's pheromones. Spying Liam's oversize shirt on the floor I pulled it on. Thankfully, it was long enough to cover my still pulsing erection. I cast a quick glance around the room noting the dramatic improvements in the cabin. The males had been busy. My mood soured further. "Do you know what Nathan will do to any male that touches his female?"

Both Mason and Liam froze.

I glared at them. "He'll rip their heart out of their chest and eat it."

Mason gulped while Liam shuddered. No one got between a Lykos Alpha male and his female and lived to talk about it.

Havana sat up in the bed with the comforter clutched to her chest. "Nathan doesn't care about me."

Seriously, how dense can she be? "Right, and that's why he ordered us to rescue you. Only you. Think about it. There are over a hundred thousand souls in Saguaro Valley and his only thought was to save you and his daughter."

Havana opened her mouth and promptly closed it.

Liam shook his head, refusing to believe what his senses had to be telling him. "She's human, Gabe. She can't be his mate."

I gave him a hard look. "Use your head, brother. Why do you think you and Mason are reacting to her like this?"

Liam took a step away from Havana and blinked as if he was seeing her for the first time. "She's a latent."

"Ding, ding. Point goes to the Enforcer with the death wish," I said in a dry voice. "She's also close to her first transition. You can smell it all over her."

Both Mason and Liam inhaled deeply and groaned.

"What's a latent?" Havana asked, sniffing her hair.

Mason and Liam looked at me for guidance. Disclosing anything about our kind with a non-Lykos was punishable by death.

"Are you 100 percent certain about this?" Liam asked.

"I thought she was an Atavus," Mason added, insinuating himself into our private mental channel.

"She's a latent," I said firmly. I replayed my recent conversation with Nathan for them starting with my cell phone ringing back at the lodge.

"Is Havana safe at Sanctuary?" Nathan's deep voice boomed as soon as I brought the phone to my ear.

"Yes."

"Good," Nathan said, relief in his voice.

In the background, I could hear his young daughter calling out, "Vana! Vana!"

Nathan made a shushing noise. "Quiet, Mira. You'll see her soon."

"You didn't tell me Havana was a latent," I said in an accusatory tone.

Nathan's silence confirmed my suspicion.

"Does Havana know what she is?"

Nathan let out a heavy sigh. "No. She knows nothing. When I first interviewed her for the nanny position, I sensed there was some Lykos blood in her—it's why I hired her in fact—but I assumed she was an Atavus. My visceral attraction to her should've been a clue that she was so much more. It wasn't until I dug into her background that I discovered she was a latent. Apparently, her mother had a one-night stand with a colonel before becoming pregnant with Havana."

My gut did a slow churn. "I'm guessing not just any colonel."

"I suspect he was one of the original test subjects from the Lykos project."

I cursed. The originals were the strongest and most unstable of our species. Tasha was a case in point. Very few had survived the military's attempt at exterminating them. Apparently, Havana's missing father had been one of the rare few the army had retained. To have survived and risen so high in rank, he must be one badass motherfucker. "You know we're required to report any suspected Lykos to Tasha and—"

Nathan interrupted me. "Tasha can't know about Havana. I'd planned to take her and Mira somewhere far from her territory."

"Well, obviously that didn't pan out. Havana's close to her transition so you'd best not take too much time getting back here. I can barely keep Liam and Mason away from her as it is." I peered out the lodge window searching in vain for the truck or the SUV. The males had been gone too long.

"She's mine!" Nathan's roar was deafening. "I will eviscerate any male that touches her. Understand?"

I pulled the phone away from my ringing ear. "Understood."

"Good," grunted Nathan. "The storm is closing in and I won't risk the drive up the mountain with Mira. Sunridge is here on our left. I'm pulling into the resort. Mira and I'll stay here for the night. Expect us first thing in the morning."

"Yes, sir," I replied before the line went dead.

Mason and Liam paled in response to the replayed conversation.

"Now do you understand?"

Both men nodded, looking stricken.

"Why do I get the feeling that you're all having a conversation I can't hear?" Havana asked from the bed.

"Because we are," I said quietly.

I could hear her heartbeat speeding up. "You guys aren't human, are you?"

I let out a weary sigh. "No."

"Then what are you?" she asked in a breathless voice. "Vampires?"

Liam let out a barking laugh.

I shook my head. "I can assure you there is nothing super-natural about us. We're man-made."

"Man-made," Havana repeated, looking to Mason for answers. For some reason that bothered me. A lot.

Mason gave her an agonized look and took a step toward her. "Havana—"

"Mason, you need to leave," I said interrupting him. I then looked over at Liam. "The same goes for you, brother. I don't want to have to bury pieces of you tomorrow."

Mason stiffened. *"Finding out you're Lykos when you've been raised as a human can be traumatic. Let me talk to her—"*

"Leave now, Dr. Wheeler and Enforcer Murphy." The steel in my voice left nothing up for debate.

Both men headed straight for the door. "Goodbye, Havana," they both said in unison before leaving. A minute later I heard the sound of their vehicles crunching through the snow.

Havana stared at me with a mixture of curiosity and apprehension in her gaze. "Are you going to tell me what you guys are?"

"No. I'm going to show you," I said, yanking Liam's shirt off my head.

Her gasp at my nakedness shouldn't have affected me the way it did. My first mistake was in looking over at her and seeing her gaze focus on my swelling shaft. The second mistake was in taking a deep steadying breath through my nose. The scent of her pheromones hit me like a punch to the gut.

I fisted my hands to keep from pouncing on her. *I can't touch her. I can't touch her.* I slammed my eyes shut trying to block out the vision of her sitting up on the bed, her gorgeous bare legs visible.

She moaned as if she was picking up on my lust. "What's happening to me? I'm not normally a nympho like this, but it's like I can't help myself. First it was Mason, then Liam, and now I want you."

Hearing that she desired me shook my resolve. *She belongs to Nathan.* Gritting my teeth, I slowly opened my eyes. "You're about to go through your first transition."

Her dark brown eyes widened. "Transition into what?"

"Into this." I slid my eye patch down so the elastic settled around my neck and shed my human form in a snapping and popping of bones and joints. My eye radiated extreme pain as it fought to regenerate around the diamond in my eye socket, but I kept my muzzle lifted until the flesh and sinew grew around the stone, holding it in place.

Havana let out a gasp as I rose as a wolf. "Oh my God." She swayed on the bed and for a moment I thought she'd pass out.

Quickly, I transformed back to human.

"You're werewolves," she cried, scrambling toward the edge of the bed away from me.

I held my hands out. "I'm not going to hurt you. And we prefer the term Lykos. Our species originated as part of a military genetic engineering project that began nearly a hundred years ago."

"The military created you?" Havana asked, some color returning to her face.

I nodded. "Yes. They wanted stronger, faster, more resilient soldiers so they created animal hybrids." *Among other abominations.* "Unfortunately, they couldn't eliminate our most primal urges, which made us unsuitable in combat and the Lykos project was deemed a failure." The urge to mate and serve our females had been both our damnation and our salvation. "Numerous members of our species managed to escape from the labs and establish factions all over this country. We've existed in secrecy ever since."

Havana blinked, taking this all better than I would've expected. "So, obviously you don't need a full moon to transform."

"No. And silver doesn't kill us although it inhibits our ability to change form," I said, anticipating her next question. I waited for her to put the pieces together and ask where she fit into all this, but instead she turned her attention to my right eye.

"Why do you have a jewel in your eye socket?"

With a start I realized I hadn't put my eye patch back in place. I grabbed it from around my neck and quickly hid the yellow diamond from view. "I wear it as punishment." Bitterness crept into my tone. "When taking our wolf form we can regenerate from most injuries, but Tas—the person who punished me doesn't want me regenerating my eye."

Havana made a sound of sympathy. "That must be painful. Why don't you take it out?"

"I can't." Tasha made sure of that with a heavy dose of compulsion. She intended the stone to be a lifelong reminder never to be blinded by loyalty to anyone other than her. Needing to change the topic, I gave Havana a penetrating look, "You're Lykos too."

Her mouth fell open, and then she laughed. "Me? A werewolf?" She shook her head. "No way."

"How old are you?"

She blinked, clearly not expecting that question. "Twenty-two."

I nodded. "A late bloomer."

"What do you mean?"

"We normally go through our first transition between eighteen and twenty-one. Females are later than males."

She rubbed her arms as if she was cold. "The first transition—that's the first time a person transforms into a wolf."

"Yes, and for females, it's the first time they go into heat."

"Heat?"

"Yes, during which time they are filled with the insatiable urge to mate."

A blush spread across her cheeks. "And that's what you think is going on with me?"

I nodded. "Nathan confirmed you're a latent when I spoke with him earlier today."

She blanched. "Nathan? He's a Lykos too?"

"Yes. He's an Alpha male, which means he's dominant over the rest of us." *But he's still under Tasha's rule.*

"And he knew I was a werewolf?"

The rising tension in her voice made me soften my tone. "He knew you had Lykos blood. He said it was one of the reasons he hired you as his daughter's nanny."

"Motherfucker." Her eyes flashed with anger. She jumped off the bed and the comforter fell to the floor. "When I see that bastard again I'm going to kick him in the balls. I can't believe he would keep this from me along with all the other crap he put me through." She stalked over and glared up at me. "And you—you've been an ass to me since the moment we met. What did I ever do to you?"

Struck dumb by the proximity of her delectable curves, I tried to take a deep steadying breath. *Fuck.* I'd forgotten to breathe through my mouth. The scent of her filled my senses, making my shaft jump at attention. "You haven't done anything, princess. Liam and Mason aren't the only ones losing their minds over you. I'm pissed because I can never have you."

She glanced down at my erection and froze. The air between us crackled with electric tension. A change seemed to come over her like a switch was hit. Her face flushed, her eyes lightened with desire, and she licked her lips. "You want me."

There was no point in denying it so I stood there like a fool.

"Well you're in luck because I want you too," she purred. "I don't care if it's some kind of werewolf heat, all I know is that if I don't get you inside me in the next five minutes, I might combust."

"I can't," I groaned.

"Why not?" she asked cupping her breasts and offering them to me. "Don't you like what you see?"

I groaned at the gorgeous sight of her stiffening peaks. "Fuck, yes. But Nathan forbade any of us from touching you. He'll kill us if we do."

A naughty smile crept across her lips. "What if I touch you instead?" She reached out and caressed my shaft with her uninjured hand.

Yesss. The feel of her soft skin against mine made my eyes roll back in my head. *No.* "I can't. I won't," I repeated, but my traitorous body refused to move away from her touch. My instincts cried out to submit to this, to her.

She slid her hand back and forth in a practiced motion that had me clenching my jaw so tight my molars ached.

Feels so good. With a ragged gasp, I rocked against her palm. *It's been so long since a female chose me.* Savage need ripped through me along with the urge to pick her up, throw her on the bed, and bury myself balls deep inside her. *Can't. Nathan.*

Before my control frayed further, I pulled away, tore open the door, and ran like a coward into the storm.

❄ 14 ❄

HAVANA

Stunned by Gabriel's sudden departure, I followed him out the open door. Ignoring the freezing air on my bare skin, I called after him, "Gabr—" I choked at the sight of him morphing from man to wolf. *Oh, God.*

The brown wolf dashed away from the cabin as if the fires of hell were licking at his paws.

He's a fucking werewolf. They're all werewolves. And I may be one too. With a cry, I stumbled back into the welcoming heat of the cabin and slammed the door. *How can any of this be possible?* My head swam with what I'd seen while my lower body still throbbed with desire.

The burning hunger inside me wouldn't let me focus on Gabriel's earth-shattering revelations nor would it allow me to feel ashamed of the way I'd gone after the man...wolf... whatever he was. Another wave of heat flashed through me.

Dazed, I stumbled to the bed on shaky legs and sat down on the mattress. The same mattress where I'd offered myself to both Liam and Mason. I inhaled deeply catching the masculine scent of the men.

Visceral need pulsed through me. If Gabriel hadn't shown

up, Liam and Mason might've taken me in every way two lusty men could take a woman. One wicked fantasy after another flashed through my mind. Mason sliding into me from behind while I took Liam in my mouth. Both men entering me at the same time...

With a moan, I fell back on the bed. The hot throb between my legs ached to the point of pain. Unable to stop myself, I stroked my damp flesh. My thighs shook as I imagined Mason flicking his tongue along my clit while Liam suckled my nipples.

Oh, God. Heat built to an inferno inside me. My entire body shuddered, and I came with a scream. Stars burst behind my eyelids as I crested on the aftershocks of the orgasm. It took a full minute before I came to my senses again. *Jesus. What's going on with me?* Gabriel said I was going through some kind of heat. Like a freaking dog, or more appropriately a wolf.

I shook my head. *Nope.* That couldn't be what was happening. *There has to be some kind of rational explanation.*

A log in the woodstove made a cracking noise.

Startled, I sat up so fast in the bed that my back spasmed. *Ouch.* I rubbed the base of my spine. It was definitely time for another pain pill. *Now where did I put them?* I glanced around the small room and frowned when I didn't spot the bottle.

Wait. What if the pills Mason gave me made me feel this way? I fisted the bed sheets. *Ibuprofen my ass.* He probably slipped me an aphrodisiac. That would explain why I'd been acting like a nympho. The drugs probably made me hallucinate too. All this business about werewolves wasn't real. My desperate need to have sex wasn't real either.

Letting out a relieved breath, I walked over to where my dress lay crumpled near the recliner. Cursing Mason under my breath, I put on the back brace and the rest of my clothes. Then I glanced over at the crate Liam had brought in. *The food might be drugged too.*

You're losing it, Vana. I rubbed my arms. *Okay, so it was unlikely that the men drugged the food.* My stomach growled in agreement. With a sigh, I padded over to the crate of food and grabbed an unopened box of chocolate chip cookies. Normally, I counted carbs like a freak, but there was nothing normal about anything in my life right now.

I carried my loot over to the recliner and stuffed my face until I couldn't fit another bite into my mouth. Another loud pop came from inside the stove reminding me I had to add more wood. I opened the door to the stove and hefted in a log. As I threw it, a sliver of wood caught on my bandage and pulled part of the gauze into the stove.

I screamed as the gauze caught on fire. Like a flash, I unwrapped my hand and threw the rest of the bandage into the stove. *Crap.* That was a close call. As I glanced down at my hand, my heart skipped a beat. Black veins trekked out like spiderwebs from the cut on my palm all the way to my wrist. My hand looked just like Dr. Sullivan's chest. *No. God, no.* Stark terror whipped through me as I rushed over to the water cooler and washed my hands. The blackened area didn't wash away. Somehow I'd gotten infected.

My mind ever so helpfully played back the memory of my fight with Brody in the club alley. The drug dealer's infected blood must've gotten into the cut on my hand.

Horrified, I probed the flesh around the wound. It was completely numb to the touch. *The dark veins will spread and I'll die just like the professor. Then I'll turn into a monster like Jess and her undead friends.*

No. I shook my head to dispel that awful thought. *Maybe I'm just hallucinating this like the whole werewolf thing.* I clenched my eyes shut and then slowly opened them. The veins were still there. My stomach rolled. *I don't think this is a hallucination. Oh, Jesus. What do I do?*

My insides tied themselves into knots as I paced. According to Mason's estimate, I'd be dead within twenty-four hours. *Unless...* Unless the doctor had a cure or a way of treating the infection. Although my trust in him was shaken, he was my only chance at survival. I glanced at the door. I couldn't wait around for him to make an appearance, assuming he even would. Mason said their place was just a few miles up the road. *I'll have to walk there.*

I slung on my boots and my jacket that Mason must've brought back inside, grabbed my duffel bag, and opened the door. A freezing gust of wind blew in a flurry of snow that covered the table and bench. *Looks like that winter storm is here. Shit.* I had no choice but to chance it. Shivering, I stepped outside.

Snow was falling fast and hard. I blinked as a white flake stuck to the top of my eyelash. Despite the howling wind and the fact I was facing almost certain death, a childlike wonder hit me. *Snow!* I'd read about it and seen it in shows but it was nothing like actually experiencing it for the first time. Mom had never taken me anywhere outside of Saguaro Valley and in the six years since her death, I'd made no effort to travel or leave town.

Regret clawed at me. I'd been so consumed with working and stocking away money for fear that I'd end up like my mother—spinning around a pole until she'd gotten too sick to dance.

Standing there as death stalked closer with every heartbeat, I realized that I'd wasted so much of my life. In the end, money didn't matter, but experiences and memories did. What precious memories did I have other than the handful of months I'd spent with Nathan, a man who'd never really loved me?

I studied the cold quiet beauty of the surrounding forest. I'd been missing out on so much. *If I survive this infection, I won't let fear and heartbreak keep me from living my life to the fullest.*

Filled with resolve, I stumbled up the steep hill following the fading tire tracks. Although trudging through snow in stilettos would've been challenging in the best of conditions, trying to do it with a broken heel made it downright treacherous.

Halfway up, I slipped on a patch of ice and fell hard on the ground. Pain like nothing I'd ever experienced radiated through my lower back. Crying out, I tried to roll to my side. Agony pinned me to the icy road. I couldn't move. *Crap!* "Help!" I screamed. "Mason! Liam! Gabriel!" I shouted their names until my voice went raw.

"They'll come along soon," I told the leaden sky. The cold crept in along with increasing wind. *Damn. This isn't good.* Teeth chattering, I tried to cover as much of my skin as I could with my thin coat. I dug through my bag with trembling hands and draped myself with my dance outfits and then finally even the bag itself.

Snow fell harder, blanketing me in fine powder. "I don't think I like you anymore," I said to the white stuff. I blew on my fingers trying to shake the feeling they were being jabbed with needles.

My nose and exposed legs burned. *Shit. I'm freezing to death.* With that realization, tears leaked from my eyes. *This is so screwed up.* I wasn't religious, but it seemed ridiculous that the powers that be would get me out of so many dangerous situations in my short life only to have me end up as a frozen corpsicle on a mountain.

It's not fair. There were so many things I'd never gotten to do. I'd never been to the beach. Gone up in a hot air balloon. Had a child. And now I never would. A wave of grief washed over me. I'd also never get the chance to find out what Nathan wanted to tell me.

Since I was dying and all, I grabbed my cell phone with my shaking fingers and pulled up the last photo I'd taken of him. Seeing his rugged face made me shiver harder. He wasn't model gorgeous in the way Gabriel, Mason, and even Liam were. His rough-hewn features were too brutal to be called handsome, but there was a compelling intensity to him that made everyone turn and stare when he walked through the room. He was one of those rare forces of nature that had the ability to put everyone he met into orbit around him.

I'd fallen under his spell from the moment he interviewed me for the nanny position. He was the whole package. Rich businessman. Doting single father. Sexy, intense, alpha male. *Ha. Little did I know there was more to that.* One look from him melted me into warm toffee, and I hadn't been coy about my attraction to him. But no matter how seductive I'd been, he'd refused to touch me until that fateful day when Max called me on my night off and begged me to sub for some dancers with the canine flu. I'd changed into my sexy dominatrix outfit and stormed the stage only to find a pair of shocked golden eyes out in the audience. After staring at Nathan like a deer in the headlights, I did the only thing I could do. Never taking my gaze from his, I gave the most seductive, lust-inducing set of my life. And when it was over, Nathan followed me offstage. Then he pinned me to the wall and kissed me so passionately, I forgot to breathe.

"I can't fight this," he'd groaned. *"I need you, Havana."*

The memory of the rest of that night made my heart pound. After an arousing threesome with his friend, he'd taken me over and over and it hadn't been enough. It never was enough with Nathan. We'd been inseparable, until that horrible Sunday evening when my world came crashing down.

My mind curled into itself as I relived the moment I'd

walked up to Nathan's front door in the rain. Knowing Mira was already asleep, I'd worn a sexy trench coat with nothing beneath. I'd rapped softly on the knocker and struck a sexy pose as he'd opened the massive oak door.

I licked my lips knowing how much he enjoyed role-playing. "Hi, sexy stranger. My car broke down and it's raining. Can I use your phone?"

There was no answering heat in his golden gaze. "Didn't you get my text?"

Taken aback by the coldness in his voice I stammered, "N-no. I forgot to charge my phone. It's dead."

"You shouldn't be here."

"But it's Sunday," I'd said like an idiot. We'd always gotten together on Sunday nights.

A feminine voice called from inside the house. "Nathan, who is it?"

"No one," he'd called back his expression hardening.

A sick feeling twisted my gut. *That doesn't sound like the housekeeper.* "Who's that?"

"Mira's mother. You need to go."

I gasped in shock. "I thought she was dead."

He'd clenched his jaw. "Go. Don't come back here or try to see me or Mira again."

His words lacerated me. Of all the ways I'd expected the night to end, no part of me was prepared for him to end our relationship. I gasped through the soul-crushing pain desperately wanting it to be some kind of bad joke.

"Why are you wasting time talking to that human trash?" a tall, blonde woman asked from over Nathan's shoulder. She was breathtakingly beautiful in a designer gold satin gown that hugged every curve of her lush body. An unearthly glow seemed to radiate from her tawny skin.

I pushed back my wet hair self-consciously feeling dull and drab next to her.

Nathan stepped between us. "Her car broke down and she wanted to use the phone."

The woman's striking yellow eyes bore into me with a predatory intensity that had me freezing in place. I'd only ever seen three pairs of eyes like hers in my life. Tyberius's, Nathan's, and the little girl who'd become like a daughter to me. "Invite her in then," the woman purred. "She could be... amusing."

Nathan tensed. If I didn't know better, I'd swear an expression of fear crossed his face. He twisted around to look at her. "No. I want you all to myself."

My stomach rolled. *God, could this get any worse?*

"Fine then," the blonde said, leaning over and nibbling the bottom lobe of his ear. "I'll be waiting for you in our bed." With that, she sashayed in the direction of Nathan's bedroom and the oversize king bed that, just two nights ago, we'd nearly broken in half with our lovemaking.

I felt all the blood leave my face. "I thought you... me..." I gasped, tears stinging my eyes.

He glanced back at me, his lip curling in distain. "You meant nothing to me."

Nothing to me. Nothing to me.

The freezing wind seemed to carry the echo of Nathan's door slamming in my face. I jolted back into the present. Shivers racked my body making my teeth snap together so hard it felt like my jaw would break. I tried to curl into a fetal position, but soon a welcome numbness settled over me. A few minutes later, I barely felt the cold. The phone slipped from my hands. *Goodbye, Nathan.*

He didn't matter anymore. Nothing mattered anymore. I was tired. So very, very tired. Losing the battle with my heavy eyelids, I succumbed to the darkness.

❧ 15 ❧

MASON

My mind was a jumbled mess as I followed Liam's truck through the gates of Sanctuary and parked the SUV near the front of the lodge. *Havana's a latent. She's one of us.* Excitement coursed through me. Like me she'd be an outsider among Lykos since those of us who were raised by humans were viewed with suspicion. Long ago, I'd stopped giving a damn about what they thought. I belonged in the human world. *With Havana.*

But she belongs to another…

My heart sank. Although I'd never been a fighter, I'd battle tooth and nail for her. The memory of her sultry moans and the sweetness of her lips made me shift in my seat. I wanted her more than I'd wanted anything in my life. And that included finding my birth family.

But Havana doesn't just belong to another Lykos male. She belongs to an Alpha. My shoulders sagged. I had no chance competing with Nathan. *Or did I?* My head shot up as I remembered our earlier conversation. Havana called him a bastard. She said she'd never take him back.

Hope flared inside my chest. The rules of our faction were

clear. Females chose their mates. Tasha was many things—psychopath, sadist, and master manipulator, but her stance on female dominance never wavered. Males served females, never the other way around. Sadly, this wasn't always the case among other factions, but in Tasha's territory Nathan would have to recognize Havana's choice.

But what if he compels her to choose him? No. I shook my head dispelling that abhorrent thought. To force a female's affection would be an act too low for any Lykos Alpha male. Although I didn't know Nathan well, I'd heard he was honorable.

Hope returned and on its heels happiness. *She'll be mine.* Filled with resolve, I jumped out of the vehicle only to find Liam exiting the truck. I froze and watched the big male walk over to me. *What if she chooses Liam instead?* The male was bigger, stronger, and could break me in a half and not break a sweat. Doubt chewed at the edges of my joy.

Liam looked shaken as he walked over. "What do you think Nathan will do to us when he finds out we were with Havana?"

"Nothing," I said as we walked up the steps.

Liam punched in the code on the panel by the door and gave me an incredulous look. "How do you figure?"

"It was her choice."

Liam rubbed his beard thoughtfully as we walked into the lodge. He strode into the library and sat down heavily on a dark leather couch. A broad smile stretched across his face. "You're right. He can't punish us if it's what Havana wanted."

I nodded. "And if she were to choose me over him, there's nothing he could do about it."

Liam jumped to his feet. "Why do you think she'd choose you? She wanted to mate with me."

A low growl rose from my throat. "She wanted me first and if you hadn't intruded, we would've mated."

Liam straightened his shoulders and looked down at me. "Clearly, you weren't her first choice because as soon as I got there she was eye-fucking me."

"Really? And that's why she asked me to join your little make-out session? Obviously, she wanted a man with more...experience."

Liam flinched and then schooled his face into a grimace. "She seemed plenty happy with what I had to offer." He reached down and grabbed his crotch.

The crass move had me fisting my hands. "Why would she want to mate with a brainless barbarian when—"

"Enough, you two. She wanted to mate with all of us," Gabriel interjected from the doorway. The male shook the snow off his naked body in a decidedly canine move. "She had her hands all over me before I could run out of the cabin."

Liam and I both growled at him.

Gabriel snarled back. "Fuck off if you know what's good for you. The female's coming up on her first heat and she'll fuck any male that gets within a few feet of her. Hell, I remember my father and I having to tie my sister down during her first heat. She kept trying to escape so she could mate with the neighbors." Uncaring of his nakedness, he padded into the library and studied a wall of books. "No matter how much each of us wants her, she belongs to Nathan. None of us can touch her." He spun around and glared at Liam and me. "Do you understand?"

Momentarily distracted by the gold gem embedded in his eye socket, I didn't respond. *The pain has to be excruciating.* The temptation to remove the foreign body so the male could heal was almost irresistible.

Liam shook his head. "She doesn't want Nathan."

"She hates the Alpha," I added. "She could choose to mate with one of us instead." *And maybe claim one of us too.*

"You're grasping at straws." Gabriel fitted his eye patch

over the jewel in his eye socket. "As soon as Nathan gets here, she'll fuck his brains out and all will be right with the two of them."

That thought made me gnash my teeth. *Damn it. I can't let that happen.*

From the expression on Liam's face, I could see he was thinking the same thing.

Gabriel cleared his throat. "I know you both want the female. Hell, I want her too, but we can't have her. I need your word that neither of you will set foot inside that cabin until Nathan gets here."

"Fine," Liam said, crossing his tree trunk-like arms.

I slowly nodded, not liking the idea one bit.

"Good." Gabriel clapped his hands together. "Now, I suggest we all take cold showers and then get something to eat. I'm starving."

Liam's stomach rumbled loudly. "I could eat."

As Gabriel and I chuckled at the same time, the tension between the three of us broke.

"I can prepare something for lunch," I volunteered. As an Omega, it was hard to fight the instinct to serve the two Enforcers.

Gabriel smiled. "That'd be great."

While he and Liam went upstairs, I headed to the kitchen. Once there, I tossed together sandwiches for the three of us. After setting the plates on the bar counter, I threw down several bags of American chips and dug through one of the full refrigerators for beers. It seemed wasteful that the lodge was stocked with food. But then again, one never knew when the feckless Tasha would want to visit one of her properties. I'm sure the staff felt it was better to be safe than sorry. At least we'd make sure all this food didn't go to waste.

"That looks good," Gabriel said, walking into the kitchen. Thankfully, the dark-haired male had dressed. Although

Lykos in the faction were used to public nudity, after so many years around humans, I'd never gotten comfortable with it.

"Smells good too," Liam added, following behind Gabriel. Although still shirtless, the big guy was at least wearing pants and had slicked back his wet hair.

"Eat up," I said, waving them to the bar stools. I set down the beer bottles and sat down next to them. For the next half hour we ate in companionable silence. Then Liam brought up football and the three of us got into a rousing debate over whether American football or soccer—the rest of the world's football—was better.

Conceding the argument before things got too heated, I cleaned up the dishes.

"You don't have to do that," Gabriel said with a raised brow.

"It's fine. I'm used to it," I said with a shrug. Living outside the faction, I'd gotten used to making my own meals and cleaning up after myself. Besides it gave me something to do other than pine after Havana.

"You guys have to see the theater room," Liam said, pointing to his right. "It will blow your mind."

"Lead the way," Gabriel said, standing.

"I'll be there in a few," I called after the other two males. I tossed the plates in the sink to wash later and threw out the empty potato chip bags. As I was putting the sandwich meat and mayo back in the fridge, my arm knocked over a can of soda. The memory of Havana licking the soda off me in the car flashed through my mind. My penis throbbed as I remembered how wild she'd been when I'd touched her. With a groan I fisted the can. *What's she doing right now? Is she alone and upset?* Gabriel wasn't the most tactful of males, and he probably hadn't shared the truth of her origins in a sensitive way.

Discovering I wasn't human had rocked my world. Years

later, I still remembered the denial, confusion, and fear. *Havana must be terrified.*

The need to see her and make sure for myself that she was okay gripped me. *I'll just drive up and peek in the window. If I don't go inside the cabin, I'm not technically breaking my word.* Deciding that I could be back before Gabriel and Liam even noticed I was gone, I snuck out of the lodge. The freezing wind slammed into me as I rushed over to the SUV and started the vehicle. *Damn, this storm is bad.*

Even more worried about Havana being alone in that cabin, I drove through the gate and then hauled ass. I was almost there when the headlights of the SUV illuminated something in the road. It looked like a body. A female body.

Bloody hell. Is that...? With my heart in my throat, I hit the brakes and jumped out of the vehicle. "Havana!" I called out as I raced through the snow.

The sight of her laying curled up in a fetal position flayed me to the bone. It looked as if she'd emptied the contents of her bag on top of her in a futile attempt to stay warm. Her eyes were closed and her skin was as pale as ice. "Havana!"

She didn't respond to her name. Her heartbeat sounded sluggish to my ears. I hauled her into my arms and carried her to the cabin. *What happened? Why did she go outside?*

Shifting her weight, I opened the door. Grateful to the welcoming heat from the stove, I set her down in the middle of the bed and did a visual inspection. Trying to distance myself from my rioting emotions, I stepped into my role as a clinician and assessed her condition. Based on her appearance, she was suffering from hypothermia and frostbite. *Does she have other injuries?*

Havana's eyes fluttered open. "M-mason," she gasped.

"I'm right here. What happened?" I tried my damnedest to keep my voice steady.

"I was trying to find you guys. I slipped. My back. I c-can't feel my legs."

Did she do further damage to her spine? I knelt down and slid my hands gently around her back. *Damn it. I can't feel anything through the brace.* "How long have you been out there?"

"I don't...I don't know."

I need to get her out of these wet clothes and raise her body temperature. "Havana, why didn't you stay here where you'd be safe?"

"I n-needed help." She lifted her left hand. "I'm infected."

At first I took the blackened skin for the advanced stages of frostbite, but then I realized it was necrotic veins mottling her skin from the tips of her finger to the middle of her forearm.

The Z-virus. Shock punched me in the solar plexus. *No. It can't be.* Trying to keep my voice calm, I asked, "When were you exposed?"

"The club alley when I fought Brody." She let out a shaky breath as if speaking so many words had exhausted her. "Y-you can cure it, right?"

Shit. If she'd already gone through her first transition, she'd be fine. But she hadn't so... Panic squeezed my insides as I looked down into her hope-filled gaze. "Of course I can, love," I lied and kissed her blackened fingers.

She gave me a ghost of a smile as she drifted back into unconsciousness.

𝕾 16 𝕾

LIAM

I'd just gone into the kitchen to see what was taking Doc so long when I heard the crunch of tires on the snow outside. "He wouldn't," I snarled under my breath.

I ran out of the kitchen, down the long hallway, and out the door. Through a blizzard of snowflakes, I glimpsed the black SUV driving out the front gate.

Motherfucker. My knuckles cracked as I fisted my hand. I knew Doc wouldn't be able to stay away from Havana. *Damn it. Gabe will flip his lid when he finds out.* Not like the Enforcer didn't have his suspicions that Doc would run to her the first chance he got. *We should've expected this.*

"Gabe, Doc's gone AWOL," I mentally shouted at my friend.

"What? He gave his word."

Lykos males took oaths seriously. But Doc was raised as a human. He wasn't like the rest of us.

Gabe cursed. *"I don't trust myself around the female. Liam, can you bring him back before he does anything stupid?"*

"Hell, yes." Unaffected by the freezing temperatures, I tore off my clothing and shed my human form. A quick snapping and popping of bones and joints and I rose as a gigantic wolf.

I shook my shaggy red fur and let out a howl of warning for Doc. That fucker needed an ass kicking. No doubt he thought to take advantage of Havana's heat to mate with her and entice her to claim him.

Fuck that. I could almost taste her exotic scent in the wind. If she's going to claim anyone, it's going to be me. After scaling the stone wall in one leap, I picked up the pace, my panting breath fogging the freezing air. It was nearly dark and the flurry of snow further reduced visibility. Still, I had no trouble picking out the shape of the SUV stopped in the middle of the road. Puzzled, I ran around the still-running vehicle noting that the driver's side door had been left open. *Why did Doc jump out in such a hurry?*

The sight of woman's lingerie scattered in the snow made my blood run cold. Havana's scent was all over. *"What happened here? Doc!"* I all but screamed into the male's mind. He didn't answer. Heart pounding, I reached the front of the cabin just as Doc busted out the door.

"Stop shouting. I'm trying to treat, Havana."

A sinking feeling gripped my stomach. *"Is she hurt?"* I peered around his shoulder and spied Havana lying on the bed unmoving.

Doc closed the door blocking my view. *"She's suffering from hypothermia, frostbite, and likely a spinal injury. That's not even the worst of it."*

"What the hell happened to her?"

Doc sighed heavily. *"She was trying to come see us when she fell in the snow."*

I whined and pawed at the ground. The female was injured because she'd been trying to see us. Shame and grief tore through me. *"We'll bring her back to Sanctuary."* *Fuck Gabe.* If he had a problem with it, he could take it up with my front claws.

"We can't risk moving her with the spinal injury." Doc thrust a

hand through his blond hair and paced back and forth. *"In the very best scenario the injury to her back will heal and she'll only lose the tip of her nose and a few fingers."*

Fuck. I lifted my head. *"I'll go back to the infirmary and get you everything you need to treat her here."*

"It wouldn't do any good." Doc gave me a bleak look. *"She's also infected with the Z-virus."*

"What? That's impossible." I shook my head refusing to believe it. *"She's Lykos. She's immune."*

Doc looked over at the door. By the expressions playing out on his face, the male was struggling with his emotions. *"She hasn't gone through her first transition so she's still vulnerable to permanent injury and…"*

"Death," my inner voice finished for him. *"Shit. There has to be something we can do. You're a fucking doctor."*

Doc flinched at my accusatory tone. *"The only way she'll survive this is if she goes through the transition before the virus spreads any further."*

"Then we help her transition." I didn't know how, but there had to be a way.

Doc rubbed his temple thoughtfully. There was hope in his eyes when he turned to me. *"Go back to the infirmary and get me all this."* He sent me images of various medical supplies and bags of blood. *"Hurry."*

"I'm on it." My blood pounded in my ears as I bolted to the SUV and shifted back into human form. Uncaring of my nakedness, I jumped into the driver's seat and sped back to Sanctuary.

Gabe met me in the lodge doorway where I stopped briefly to throw on my jeans. "Where's Mason? You were supposed to bring him back."

I shoved the head Enforcer out of my way. Panic and worry chewed at me as I rushed into the library and opened the passage to the hidden elevator. As I stepped into the metal box, Gabe grabbed my arm.

"Where the hell are you going? Where's Mason?" When I didn't reply, he snarled. "Talk to me. I'm your fucking superior."

"There's no time," I growled, shoving the male across the room.

"You'd better make time." Gabe bared his teeth and unsheathed his claws.

I'd long wondered if I could best the legendary Enforcer in combat—his speed and cunning up against my strength and size. But this wasn't the time to find out. I sent him mental images of Havana's condition.

Gabe's anger was replaced by shock. I didn't need to read his mind to sense his worry. "We'll bring the female here."

"She's too bad off. We can't move her. I'm getting supplies for Doc. He's not sure she'll survive. She's been infected with the Z-virus."

"Fuck, no." Gabe's face paled. "How can I help?"

"Grab extra blankets. There should be plenty upstairs."

Gabe nodded and, in a rare turnabout, followed my orders. He dashed down the hallway while I took the elevator down to the infirmary. After stuffing a medical bag with all the supplies Mason needed, I stopped at the fridge in the back of the room. There were dozens of blood bags in there. *Which ones was I supposed to get?* Frantic to get back to the cabin, I grabbed a handful and rushed back to the elevator.

Gabe was just loading a pile of blankets into the SUV when I ran out the front door. Night had fallen, and the storm was raging. Gabe slid into the driver's seat while I jumped into the front passenger seat.

"Hurry!" I pleaded. Havana could be slipping further away with every minute.

Wind and snow pounded the windshield as Gabe slowly drove out of the compound.

"Step on it, brother!" I shouted.

"If you haven't noticed, the storm of the century is barreling down on us, asshole. Unless you'd like to get stuck in the snow, shut the fuck up."

It took far too much time for Gabe to pull up to the cabin. Not even waiting for the vehicle to stop, I jumped out with the bag of medical supplies. I pushed the cabin door open with such force it slammed into the wall.

Doc jumped to his feet. "There you are. Do you have everything?"

"Yes." I ran over to the bed where Doc was standing over Havana's body. He'd removed her wet clothing and bundled her in the comforter.

I stared down at the female, my insides shredding. Her beautiful dark hair fanned around her too-pale face. *She can't die.* I sucked in a breath when I caught sight of her left hand —it was black from the tips of her fingers all the way up her arm. "Is that from frostbite?"

"No." Doc slowly turned over her hand revealing dark veins spidering out from the cut on her palm. "This is where the infection originated."

The memory of Havana cutting her hand and then fighting off the creature in the alley flashed in my mind. *Fuck.* She'd been infected because I hadn't gotten to her in time. I'd failed her, and she'd pay the price.

Gabe walked over to stand beside me. He wore a resigned look on his face. "She's infected. You know what needs to be done, Mason."

"Let me try this first," Doc said, hooking a bag of blood to the collapsible IV pole I'd brought from the infirmary.

"Is that Lykos blood?"

Mason nodded.

Gabe tensed. "Don't you remember what happened the last time you tried to use Lykos blood to cure the virus?"

Mason paled. "This is different. She's one of us."

Gabe gritted his teeth. "No. She hasn't gone through her first transition. Our blood will kill her. Maybe you don't care if she suffers, but I won't watch her bleed out in front of me. I'll show her mercy even if you won't." Gabriel reached for his gun, only to find it missing. Seeming to remember he'd given it to me back on the interstate, he looked over. "Go get my gun."

I shook my head. "Let Doc do his thing."

"She'll die in excruciating pain," Gabe muttered as we watched Doc find a vein on Havana's right arm and start the infusion.

Gabe's wrong. He has to be wrong. I held tightly to that hope as the minutes went by. The flames from the open woodstove danced over Havana's still face while the wind beat against the windows outside.

The roaring storm shook the tiny cabin.

"Let's hope it holds," Gabe said as we looked up at the roof.

An anguished cry made us both jerk our heads toward Havana.

"It's working," Doc shouted, yanking the IV out of Havana's arm.

Gabe and I both stepped forward to see Havana thrashing on the bed.

"She's succumbing to the blood poisoning," Gabe cried with a tortured expression on his face.

A familiar popping noise rang out.

"No, she's transitioning," Doc said, pointing down at Havana.

Before our eyes her jaw and nose lengthened into a muzzle and her body took a lupine shape under the comforter. In less than a minute an enormous black wolf lay panting on the bed.

I blinked in surprise. *She's massive.* Although I was one of the biggest wolves in the faction, this creature dwarfed me. She might've been bigger than even Tasha.

"What the...?" Gabe murmured.

At the sound of his voice, the black wolf opened her eyes. The bright gold gaze of an Alpha female pinned us to the floor.

"What did you do to me?" Havana's hysterical voice rang through our minds. *"Why am I like...like this?"* She frantically gnawed at the comforter with her razor-sharp teeth.

"It's okay, Havana. You're okay," Doc repeated in a steady voice from behind her.

She scrambled to her feet, her paws tangling in the bedding. *"I'm not okay!"* she screamed into our minds. *"I'm a goddamn wolf!"*

"Settle down," Gabe ordered.

She snarled and snapped her teeth at his face.

I stepped in front of my friend and held out my hands to the massive wolf. "Shh. Calm down."

She blinked those large gold eyes at me, snaring my soul. *"What's going on, Liam? Tell me!"* Her plea rang through my mind with so much power it made me clutch the sides of my head in agony.

Gabe gasped. "She's compelling you."

Before I could respond, Doc plunged a syringe into the wolf's neck.

Havana twisted around. Her pointed ears flattened as she snarled at the blond male. She took a step toward him and stumbled. A heartbeat later her head drooped, and she collapsed back on the mattress.

Doc wiped the sweat from his brow and looked up at us. "I gave her a sedative."

Slowly the dark fur on Havana's body disappeared as she shifted back into human form. She'd healed completely. No black veins or cuts marred the skin of her hand and arm. Her thrashing had thrown off most of the comforter and the sight of her bare breasts and the tempting cleft between her legs made my breathing hitch. She was the most beautiful creature I'd ever laid eyes on. *And she's one of us now.*

Noticing that Gabe was also staring, I growled.

Doc readjusted the comforter, hiding her body from sight.

"She's an Alpha," Gabe said incredulously. "How is that possible?"

"It's not," I replied. Everyone knew the rarest of our kind were born, not made, something Tasha reminded us of all the time. If Havana were an Alpha female, she would've had bright yellow eyes from birth.

Doc shook his head. "I'd theorized the transfusion of Lykos blood would accelerate her transition and healing, but I never expected this." He walked over and inspected the bag of blood still hanging on the IV pole. He looked over at me, his eyes widening. "You brought me Tasha's blood, Liam."

"I-I didn't look at whose it was. I just grabbed a few bags," I stammered. *Shit. What have I done?*

"Damn it." Gabe scrubbed a hand over his face. "You know what Tasha will do to another Alpha female in her territory."

She'll kill her in the most painful way possible. I swallowed hard. *"By saving Havana's life, we've condemned her to death."*

"No, we haven't." Doc's voice rang inside my head. *"I swore to keep Havana safe and I intend to keep that oath. I won't let Tasha hurt her."*

"Neither will I," I declared, deciding then and there that this female was more important than anything else, including my family at Winterhaven and my own life.

"And neither will I," Gabe added.

Mason and I gaped at the head Enforcer. Never would I have expected treasonous words to come from his lips.

"Tasha lost my loyalty when she destroyed my family." Gabe looked at us with a fierce expression on his face. *From now on, I serve a new Alpha female.*" He bowed his head in the direction of Havana, and then got to his knees beside the bed.

Doc and I followed suit. As we took turns verbally pledging ourselves to her sleeping form, we established a new faction. We just needed to keep our ruler alive so she could lead it.

❧ 17 ❧

HAVANA

pinprick in my arm woke me. "Ouch." I tried to move and found I couldn't. A hand held me down. *What the hell?* Adrenaline spiked my blood. *Where am I? What's happening?* The smell of rubbing alcohol assaulted my senses.

"Just relax," said a familiar accented male voice.

Mason. All at once the tension eased out of my body.

I opened my eyes to find the handsome blond doctor standing over me. As I looked up, he pulled a needle out of my arm. "What are you giving me?" My voice sounded dry and raspy.

"Something to rouse you. You've been unconscious for several days."

"Several days," I echoed feeling dazed. The fluorescent lights above me burned my eyes. The buzzing noise from what resembled a refrigerator in the corner of the room rang in my ears like a chorus of cicadas. My head swam as I tried to knit together the fragments of my recent memories. I remembered falling in the snow. It'd been so cold. And the black veins on my hand. "I'm infected," I cried out, pushing Mason away.

The doctor flew into the next hospital bed. He looked as stunned as I did. "Easy there. You're no longer infected with the Z-virus."

I looked at my hand. There wasn't a trace of the virus there, nor was there even evidence of the cuts on my palm. "H-how?"

Ignoring my question, he studied me with a pensive expression on his face. "What's the last thing you remember?"

"You finding me and bringing me back to the cabin." I paused and looked around at the white-on-white space that could double as a triage room in any hospital. "Which we clearly aren't at anymore. Where are we?"

"We're at Sanctuary. Well, more specifically, the infirmary at the lodge." Mason bent down and recovered the syringe that had flown from his hand to the floor. He turned and disposed of it in a red container on the counter by a stainless steel sink.

A sink meant running water and that meant showers and toilets. Thank God. "Okay," I said slowly. "I thought Gabriel didn't want me staying here."

Mason flashed me a strained smile. "Your almost dying changed his mind. From now on you stay with us." He walked back over to my side. "All your injuries should be healed. How does your back feel?"

Gritting my teeth against the inevitable pain, I sat up. To my surprise, I didn't feel even a twinge of discomfort. The bed sheet tangled around me as I twisted from side to side. "My back doesn't hurt at all." I blinked in amazement. It'd been forever since I'd had this range of motion. "What did you give me?"

"A blood transfusion. The blood helped accelerate...your healing process."

I started to ask him how a transfusion could heal a person so dramatically when he brought my hand to his mouth and brushed his lips across my knuckles. The sensation of his mouth against my skin made me shudder. Heat moved low into my belly and I forgot everything except for how delicious he looked in the burgundy polo he was wearing.

He inhaled deeply and groaned. "Christ, you smell amazing."

"I doubt that," I said, brushing back my tangled hair. I looked down at myself, realizing that I was wearing a hospital gown with nothing underneath. "Where are my clothes?"

"Back at the cabin. They were sopping wet. I had to remove them."

"So you stripped me naked?" I gave him a teasing grin.

"Um, yes. And I admit I gave you a sponge bath or two." Mason rubbed the back of his neck as a hint of red crept over his cheekbones. "I promise I took no liberties."

"Maybe I want you to take liberties," I said in a husky voice. Another pulse of desire swept through me. I reached out and caressed his handsome face.

His beautiful blue eyes widened. "You shouldn't touch me."

Oh, I would touch him. *All over.* Licking my lips, I reached back and undid the ties at the back of the gown, baring myself to his gaze.

"No," Mason whispered. As if on their own volition, his hands reached for me. At the last minute he pulled them back and took a step away. "I can't."

"Yes, you can." My core throbbed, aching to be filled. "I need you, Mason."

Mason swallowed hard. "I promised the others."

At that moment, I didn't care about anyone else but him. "This is about you and me." I tore off the hospital gown and slid to the end of the bed. "Come to me." My voice rang with a strange unworldly tone.

Wearing a dazed look, he walked straight into my embrace.

I wrapped my bare legs around his waist and kissed the column of his throat. His fresh rain scent teased my senses, making me burn even hotter for him. When he didn't move, I whispered, "Kiss me."

He lowered his head and claimed my lips in a drugging kiss.

"Touch me," I whispered against his lips. I placed one of his hands on my breast.

He caressed my nipple.

Moaning, I arched into his palm. "Harder."

He pinched the hardening peak making me cry out in pleasured pain.

"Yes," I hissed as he did the same to my other nipple. "Now here." I slid his hand between my legs.

He sucked in a shaky breath and stroked my damp folds. "Bloody hell."

I moaned and bucked under his touch. "Ah, yes there."

His eyes seemed to glaze over as he found my clit.

"Yes, yes," I cried as he worked my nub. My thighs quaked as pleasure streaked through me. "More."

He slid two fingers inside me and I nearly came undone.

"Oh, God!" Unable to stay upright, I fell back over the bed.

He pushed my thighs farther apart and suddenly his mouth was on me.

I screamed his name as he thrust his tongue inside and catapulted me into a mind-shattering orgasm.

Not even letting me catch my breath, he continued his erotic assault, licking and sucking me mindless.

Quaking and trembling against his lips, I was on the razor's edge of another orgasm when there was a loud crashing sound.

"Motherfucker. Doc, you're dead."

There was a blur of motion. Mason was ripped away and hurled into one of the cabinets. Glass shattered and medical supplies flew across the room.

Mason lay on the floor staring up at the giant of a man who stood over him. "Liam, I can explain."

Liam's chest heaved. "Explain it to my fists." He picked Mason up by the throat and punched the doctor in the face.

Liam will kill him! My desire evaporated under an onslaught of fear. "Let him go!" I scrambled off the hospital bed.

Jerking his head around to look at me, Liam dropped Mason to the ground.

I rushed over to the smaller man. "Are you okay?"

He rubbed his jaw and nodded.

I glared up at Liam. "How dare you attack him!"

Liam glanced down at my naked body and swallowed hard. "He was taking advantage of you after we all swore not to touch you." He let out a rumbling growl and swung his menacing glare back at Mason.

I laid my hand on Liam's broad chest feeling the thundering of his heart against his tight knit shirt. "He didn't take advantage of me."

"She ordered me," Mason gasped, stumbling to his feet. "I couldn't resist her compulsion."

Liam froze. "Is that true?"

Confused, I looked between the two of them. "I-I told him to touch me."

"She doesn't yet know her power," a deep voice said from the doorway.

We all turned to see Gabriel leaning against the doorframe.

The dark-haired man was dressed in a black T-shirt and jeans and looked good enough to eat. "Leave us," he ordered the other men.

Neither Liam nor Mason looked happy, but they followed his order and strode from the room. Based on the dark looks Liam gave Mason, he still wasn't happy with the doctor.

After closing the door behind them, Gabriel threw something at me.

Reflexively, I caught the ball of shimmery fabric. As I pulled it apart, I discovered it was a gold silk robe.

"Put it on."

I bared my teeth at him. Something in me rebelled at him giving me an order.

Gabriel took a step back and gentled his voice. "Please put it on, Havana."

Mollified, I slid the robe around me, loving the fabric's soft slide against my skin. The owner of the robe clearly had luxurious taste. "Whose robe is this?" I asked, curiosity getting the better of me. It didn't seem like anything the men would wear.

"The Alpha female who lived here," Gabriel said, crossing his arms.

I blinked. *Not this stuff about Alphas and wolves again.*

"Why don't you sit down?" Gabriel nodded at a stainless steel stool over by the counter.

"I'd rather stand," I said stiffly, remembering the last conversation we'd had. Swallowing hard, I said, "Just be honest, did Mason drug me so I hallucinated you turning into a werewolf?"

Gabriel let out a deep laugh. "I can assure you he did not." The smile faded from his lips. "But what he did was so much worse. He gave you a transfusion of Lykos blood to push you through your first transition and in doing so turned you into an Alpha female."

I shook my head. "You can stop now. I'm not buying into the Alpha werewolf crazy talk." *Mason must've injected me with more of that aphrodisiac drug.* That's why I'd all but boned him on the exam table.

"If it only were crazy talk." Gabriel crossed the distance between us and looked down at me. "You're now a Lykos Alpha female, Havana. And with that comes a great deal of power." He gestured at my hand. "The power to shift into a wolf and heal your injuries."

I let out a weak laugh. *As if.*

His serious expression didn't change. "And the power to compel humans and other Lykos to do your bidding."

"You mean like mind control?"

"Exactly," he whispered into my mind.

"Did you just speak to me telepathically?" I cried, taking a shaky step back. My bare foot crunched down on a piece of broken glass from the cabinet. The sharp pain was a welcome distraction. I reached down and pulled the jagged shard from my heel. Blood poured from the wound.

"Heal yourself," Gabriel ordered.

I looked up at him in confusion. "How?"

"Find your wolf." He sent images of me transforming into a large black wolf.

No. I shook my head, rejecting the idea. "That's impossible."

"Don't fight it. Change!" Gabriel's voice reverberated off the walls of the room. He ripped the gold robe off me.

Instinctive fury rose inside me. *How dare he command me!* A snarl escaped my lips. Suddenly, every muscle in my body seemed to contract at once. Bones and cartilage snapped and popped. Overcome with the startling sensation of my body being remade, I fell forward and landed on huge claw-tipped black paws.

My shocked cry turned into a bark. *Holy hell. I'm a wolf.*

"Impressive. Now change back." When I blinked at him, he added, "Visualize your human form."

Once I imagined myself as I'd looked the last time I'd peered into a mirror, I immediately snapped and popped back to my real body. *Wow.* I looked at my trembling human legs with a mixture of wonder and horror.

Gabriel handed me the robe and watched me put it on. "Look, see how your foot has healed."

I glanced at my heel. There wasn't even a scar to show where the wound had been. "I don't understand." *This can't be happening. None of this can be happening.*

Seeming to sense my crisis, Gabriel grabbed my elbow and led me over to the stool. "You're different now." As I sat down heavily, he went over to the counter, picked up a stainless steel tray and held it out. "See for yourself."

I peered into the shiny bottom of the tray and blinked at the pair of bright yellow eyes staring back at me. *My eyes.* "What happened to my eyes?"

"You have the eyes of an Alpha now. I pray you won't abuse your power like others of your kind." His voice held a bitter note.

The memory of my encounter with Mason replayed in my mind. *Did I compel him to touch me?*

"Probably. Although I'm sure he wasn't unwilling."

I jumped. "You can read my mind."

"You're telegraphing your thoughts for anyone to hear. You'll have to learn to shield them."

"Can I read your thoughts?" I asked, as curiosity warred with fear.

"Try me," he said, kneeling down next to the stool.

I gazed into his dark eye.

"Please don't become like Tasha."

Shit. I can read minds now. I swallowed hard. "What did this...Tasha do to you?"

He flinched and stood. "Besides this—" he motioned at his eye patch. "She compelled me to murder my entire family."

18

GABRIEL

Havana gasped and her beautiful face paled. "She made you kill your family?"

Shame and grief filled me as the horror of that night came back. "My sister had just given birth to her first child—Isla. It should've been a joyous occasion, but the babe was born with yellow eyes marking her as an Alpha female. Even though they're revered among the other factions as the rarest and most powerful of our kind, Tasha views them as a threat to her rule."

I let out a deep breath. "I knew I should've moved them to another faction immediately, but my parents and my sister's mate wanted to wait a few days for my sister to recover from the birth. Somehow Tasha found out." I gritted my teeth as regret and pain knotted my stomach. "She confronted me, ripped the truth out of my mind, and compelled me to slay every member of my family. And I did." I clenched my eye shut as if that would block the memory of their screams.

Havana stood and laid her hand on my shoulder. "Oh, my God. That's horrible."

Shooting pain had me rubbing my eye patch. "After it was done, Tasha ripped out my eye, placed one of her diamonds in my eye socket. She compelled me to wear it for the rest of my life to remind me of my betrayal."

Havana shook her head in disbelief. "That woman's a monster, Gabriel."

That she is. "I'm sharing this with you so you'll understand the depths of your power and what you'll be up against. Because as soon as Tasha discovers what you are, she'll come for you." *She'll come for us all.*

Instead of being filled with fear, Havana's golden gaze narrowed. "Good. That bitch's reign of terror needs to end."

My heart wrenched at the mental image of Havana facing off with Tasha. Tasha would make sport of destroying her piece by piece. Then she'd mount Havana's head on her trophy wall as a warning to others. My throat tightened. *No. I can't let that happen.* I'd failed my niece and my family, but I wouldn't fail Havana. Somehow I'd figure out a way to keep Tasha from finding her.

Trying to push thoughts of the evil she-wolf from my mind, I cleared my throat. "Why don't I show you to your room while you still have your wits about you?"

"What do you mean?"

"Do you remember the first heat cycle I told you about?"

She nodded slowly.

"You'll begin it soon."

She flushed. "I think I might already be in it."

I gave her a pitying look. "Believe me, you'd know." The heat cycle was twenty-four hours of unyielding torment for females. Only the semen from a Lykos male could ease the primal assault on their bodies.

"Oh," she said breathlessly.

She was so fucking gorgeous. I tried not to notice the glimpses of her thigh peeping through the gaps in the robe or the way her pert nipples pressed against the silky fabric. I couldn't let my brain travel down that treacherous road. Not while Nathan had already staked his claim.

As if picking up on my thoughts, Havana cocked her head to the side and said, "Are Nathan and Mira here?"

"No. The storm still rages. When it clears, they'll come." I strode over to the door and opened it hoping she wouldn't detect my worry. The storm had taken out all the radio and cell towers and I hadn't been able to reach the Alpha male. I hoped the virus hadn't reached Sunridge, but if it had... There was no telling what threats he and his daughter were facing.

As we stepped out into the hallway, Liam and Mason stopped in the middle of what looked like a heated argument and rushed to Havana's side.

Mason grabbed her hand. "You must be famished. Can I make you something to eat?"

Liam pushed him away. "Why don't you make her food while I give her a tour of the lodge?"

The doctor gritted his teeth. "I was planning on giving her a tour after I've made her lunch."

Havana's wide-eyed gaze ping-ponged between them.

Trying to stifle a laugh, I held up my hand. "Enough. I'll be escorting Ms. James, to her room where she can relax and take a hot shower."

"That'd be amazing," she said, stepping around the other males.

Their crestfallen expressions were almost comical.

Havana looked back into the infirmary. "I guess all my stuff is scattered in the snow by the cabin."

"I can go get your things," Liam offered, looking like an overeager puppy.

Havana's gaze brightened. "You'd do that for me?"

"I'd do anything for you," Liam said, clasping her hand.

"As would I," Mason declared, grabbing her other hand.

Rolling my eyes, I said, "Liam, go get Havana's things. Mason, go prepare something for her to eat."

The males nodded and strode with us down the hallway to the elevator. Both males practically hung off her arms as we traveled up in the small steel box.

I sighed heavily. It was both a blessing and a curse that we males were instinctively driven to serve the needs of our Alpha female.

After promising Havana they would see her soon, Liam and Mason exited on the first floor. Havana and I continued up to the second.

Her eyes nearly bugged out of her head when we stepped out of a hidden door within a spacious walk-in closet. "What is this place?" She reached out and touched one of the dozens of shimmery designer gowns.

The cloying scent of roses clinging to the dresses made my nose wrinkle. "This is one of Tasha's vacation homes and these are her things."

Havana snatched her hand back as if burned. "I don't want to wear her clothes."

I stifled the impulse to nod approvingly. "I'm sure we can find you something else. Come." I waved her through the gold-hued bathroom and into the bedroom.

Havana stopped short, her gaze fixed on the life-size portrait of Tasha hanging over the king bed. The artist had captured the blonde female's stunning beauty along with the wild, unhinged look in her yellow eyes.

"Meet Tasha Digoski," I said, flashing Havana a bitter smile.

Havana gasped. "I know her. She's Mira's mother."

Surprised that Havana had met Tasha and lived to tell the tale, I could only nod.

Havana's eyes narrowed. "Nathan left me for her." She paused and let out a brittle-sounding laugh. "Well, I guess the truth is that he was cheating on her with me."

Even though it wasn't my place to get in the middle of Alpha politics, I had to set her straight. "Doubtful. Nathan was Tasha's consort until Mira was born. As soon as she realized the baby was an Alpha, she tried to murder her. Nathan stopped her, offering Tasha anything to save Mira's life. Since Tasha had long coveted Nathan's position on the Council, she made him a deal. The Council seat and his eternal servitude for letting the child live. I can assure you Nathan has no warm feelings for Tasha."

Havana blinked and took a minute to process my words. "She was at his house the night he broke up with me. He acted so cold when he told me to leave and never contact them again, but when I think back on it, he wasn't acting like himself."

Without trying, I glimpsed Havana's memories of that night. The Alpha male had clearly been scared out of his mind. "Nathan was probably worried that Tasha would discover your relationship. If she had, she would've killed you on the spot. Nathan ended your relationship to save your life."

Tears filled Havana's eyes as she gazed back up at the picture. "I didn't know. I hate—hated him for how he treated me."

Congratulations, asshole. She's back in love with the Alpha, my inner voice chided. *Now she'll never be mine.*

Havana jerked her head up. "I'm not back in love with him. I simply understand better what happened. If he truly loved me, he would've told me the truth about her and about the Lykos."

I felt my face redden at the fact she'd read my mind. *I'll have to better guard my thoughts.* Needing to escape the sight of Tasha and her nauseating rose scent, I led Havana out of the bedroom down the hall into a more masculine space.

Havana inhaled deeply as we walked into the room, her gaze taking in the dark mahogany furniture and oversize four-poster king bed. "This smells like Nathan."

"Yes, it was his bedroom. Tasha hasn't let anyone stay in here since he left. I thought you might like this room." *And I thought if you're surrounded by the scent of the Alpha, I'll be able to resist you.*

She flashed me a knowing look that told me she'd read my mind.

Clearing my throat, I showed her the large bathroom.

She moaned at the sight of the walk-in shower that was so large it took up an entire wall. Her hand went to the belt of her robe.

I sucked in my breath anticipating another glimpse of her body. *I want her so much.*

Havana whirled around, her face flushed. "I want you too, Gabriel." She shimmied out of the robe and I forgot to breathe.

Fuck. She was so beautiful. Her breasts were the perfect size, just big enough to fit in my hands. The tempting strip of hair between those long legs that seemed to go on forever made my shaft throb.

"Please, Gabriel," she begged.

Her intoxicating scent clouded my mind. My hands traced the underside of her breasts before I could get control.

"No." I shook my head. "There's shampoo and soap in there. I'll wait outside the room while you shower." Not waiting for her response, I rushed back out into the bedroom and then sought refuge in the hallway.

Fuck. I knew it was just her impending heat making her proposition me like that, but it was getting harder and harder to resist her pull. *What if you didn't?* an insidious voice inside my head asked. *What if you gave her what she asked for?*

I shuddered. Lust burned all rational thought from my

brain as I fantasized all the ways I'd take her. *I'll give her such pleasure she'll claim me as her own. No! That can't happen.* By some force of will, I kept myself in the hallway. Minutes or hours later, Liam and Mason joined me.

The doctor carried a tray of pasta, fruit, and soda while Liam held Havana's duffel bag in one beefy hand.

"She's taking a shower," I said, refusing to leave my post by the door. "I'll make sure she gets those when she's done."

Mason set down the tray of food and glared at me with far too much impertinence for a male who'd never had to fight for his life. "I'll wait until she gets out."

"Me too," rumbled Liam.

"Suit yourse—" I broke off when a pain-filled cry rang out. "Havana!"

I flung open the door and the three of us rushed inside.

"She's not here," Liam shouted, looking around the bedroom.

"The bathroom," I yelled, rushing toward the scent of sandalwood that hung in the steamy air. I flung open the bathroom door and my heart stopped.

Havana lay writhing on the tile floor of the shower. Catching sight of me she moaned, "Gabriel, I need you. It hurts." The hand she held between her legs told me all I needed to know.

We need to leave.

"Havana!" Mason cried trying to step by me and open the glass door.

"No." I grabbed his arm in a death grip and dragged him back.

"Is she hurt?" Liam demanded, trying to force his way into the bathroom.

I pushed both males out of the bathroom into the bedroom. "No. Well, technically yes. She's in heat."

Havana let out another cry that sliced through me like a jagged blade.

"She's in pain," Dr. Obvious stated, thrusting a hand through his hair. "We can't let her suffer like that."

Liam wore a look of helpless frustration. "How do we help her?"

A solution popped into my mind. I looked over at Mason. "We can knock her out again. Do you have more of that sedative you gave her in the cabin?"

The blond male frowned. "Given that a small amount put her out for days, I wouldn't advise giving her another dose. She may not wake at all next time."

Great. Well that option is out. "Then mating is the only thing that will relieve her pain."

"I volunteer to help her," Liam declared, marching to the door.

Mason growled. "I don't think so." He darted in front of Liam.

Liam swung his arm and sent Mason flying into a mahogany dresser. Then he reached for the bathroom doorknob.

No. She's mine. Teeth bared in aggression, I raced across the bedroom and grabbed Liam's arm. Wrenching the limb behind his back, I threw him face-first into the door.

The giant threw his head back slamming me in the forehead. "You want her for yourself, brother?"

Yes. "No." *What am I doing?* Shaking off the stars dancing in my line of vision. I released Liam. As I backed away from the giant, I glimpsed all three of us in the mirror hanging on the wall. With our eyes glowing and lips peeled back from our teeth, each of us looked ready to tear the others apart for the chance to mate with the female. *Shit. It'll get bloody unless...she chooses.* Female's choice was the status quo in Winterhaven and it should be in our new faction too. "Havana will have to choose between us."

Liam winced, likely thinking of all the times females had chosen another over him.

"What?" Mason asked, getting to his feet.

I cleared my throat knowing I'd probably regret this for the rest of my likely short life. But fuck, the female was in pain and Nathan wasn't around. Mason was right. *We can't let our Alpha female suffer.* "Havana will choose between the three of us. The chosen male will mate with her and the other two males must not interfere. Understood?"

"Yes," Liam and Mason said in unison.

The bathroom door crashed open.

We all turned our gazes to the mesmerizing sight of Havana standing naked in the doorway.

19

HAVANA

All three men stared at me slack-jawed as I clung to the doorframe for dear life.

"Help me," I panted. I brought my fist to my mouth to muffle a cry of pain as my lower belly cramped and my core spasmed with need. My knees gave out with no warning, but somehow Gabriel caught me.

"I told you you'd know when the heat hit, princess," he said with a crooked smile.

I moaned in agony. Never in my life had I experienced such unyielding lust. My sex burned, my skin felt so sensitized it could melt right off my flesh. "Please," I begged rubbing my thighs together seeking relief from the torment.

He carried me to the oversize king bed and set me on the soft velvet comforter. Tension thrummed through his body as he stepped away from me. "Which of us do you want to mate with?" He motioned between himself and the other males.

My vision was tinged in red as I looked over the men.

Liam's muscular chest rose and fell rapidly as he watched me with a mixture of hope and anxiety in his dark green gaze.

If I chose the gentle giant who'd sworn to protect me, I'd be his first woman.

Mason stood next to him, his beautiful blue eyes glinting with passion and desire. The sexy doctor would do anything to make me happy. *Anything.* And I'd already had a taste of how he could pleasure me. I licked my lips in eager anticipation.

Dragging my gaze from Mason, I focused on the man in black. Gabriel. He stood stiffly, his one dark eye fixed on the door as if he was getting ready to bolt. But I wasn't fooled. I'd read his mind. He wanted me to be his. And I wanted him to be mine.

The men seemed to hold their collective breaths as I pretended to deliberate.

Suddenly, a maelstrom of heat tore through my body. With a cry, I fell back on the bed arching in pain. "All of you," I gasped. "I want all of you."

The men became statues.

"She wants us all?" Liam asked in a confused voice.

"Yes. All of you," I screamed.

Mason let out a strained laugh. "Well, I'm willing to share, if you are."

"That's not how it's done," Gabriel chided. "One male to one female. You know the rules."

"Tasha's rules," Liam spat. "She made them so no female could be more powerful or more protected than her. Females in other factions mate with more than one male."

"True," Gabriel said, slowly turning his gaze back to me. "So, all three of us?"

"Yes," I gasped. Another wave of heat crashed into me. "Someone get over here now!" At that point, I would've screwed the freaking zombie professor if it would've stopped the pain.

Liam fumbled with his fly. "I'm coming, beautiful."

Gabriel slapped the big man in the chest. "You'll split her apart with that shit. Let one of us go first and get her ready for you."

"You can go," Mason said to Gabriel. He added in a low voice, "I, uh, just took care of myself downstairs."

What does a girl have to do to get fucked around here? I moaned, rubbing my clit furiously, but no matter how I worked myself, I couldn't come.

"I got you, princess," Gabriel said, approaching the bed.

Finally. I reached out for him with clawing hands and dragged him on top of me. "I need—I need." I couldn't get the words out. I frantically tore at his pants needing his skin on mine so badly I could taste blood.

Pushing my hands away, he freed his long, pulsing length.

I almost wept in relief. "Please!"

He brushed his thick cock back and forth against my swollen folds. Then he claimed my mouth in a possessive kiss.

Desperation tore through me. I bit his lip hard. *No kissing. No foreplay. No teasing.* Lust twisted my insides. "Get inside me," I screamed, digging my nails into his tight ass.

He gripped my hips and entered me with one thrust.

The feel of his heat sliding through my wet channel was just what my body craved. "Yes, yes!" I cried, arching up off the bed.

He thrust in and out, his thick length filling me perfectly.

"Harder!" I wrapped my legs around his waist, urging him on.

He pounded me into the mattress with savage intensity.

It was everything I craved. Everything I needed. The tension inside me ratcheted higher and higher. "Don't stop!"

He pistoned his hips, electricity sparking through me with each frenzied thrust.

"Oh, God!" Half out of my mind, I was dimly aware of him reaching between our bodies and finding my clit.

A violent orgasm tore through me, shaking every bone in my body.

Bellowing my name, Gabriel came in jerking spasms that bathed my core in his seed.

Unable to control myself, I came again and again until my vision went white. As I trembled with the aftershocks, the grinding need relented. I let out a shuddering breath and clung to his sweat-slicked back. "Thank you."

He pushed up on his elbows and looked down at me. His one dark eye still glinted with passion. "Anytime, princess." He leaned down and kissed me. "That was incredible."

I could feel the truth in his words and in the deep satisfaction that radiated from him.

I want this man for now. For always. Some primitive instinct made me whisper, "You're mine," against his lips.

He jerked back as if I'd slapped him. Then he studied my face with some unnamed emotion flashing in his intense gaze. "How I want that to be true. But I can't be yours."

Disappointment thrummed through me, easing only when he deepened the kiss, turning it into something hot and wild. "Oh, yes." *More. I needed more.*

His cock hardened as my inner walls spasmed around him.

I moaned, readying for another delicious ride when Gabriel surprised me by pulling out.

While I blinked at him in confusion, he grabbed my hips, flipped me over and pulled me up on my hands and knees. Then he entered me again in a delicious spine-tingling thrust of his hips.

I let out a shocked moan and stared into the lust-filled gazes of Liam and Mason. *How could I have forgotten about them?*

The men stood a few feet from the bed.

Mason's eyes were bright with longing as he watched Gabriel take me.

Liam had pulled out his cock and was stroking it.

My mouth dropped open when I saw its size. *Holy hell.*

As if sensing my interest in the others, Gabriel grabbed a handful of my hair and yanked my head back possessively. My back arched into the muscles of his smooth bronze chest. "Don't forget about me."

"Never!" I panted as his thrusts grew wilder. "But you need to learn to share." I motioned Liam over. "Touch me," I gasped, offering my breasts to him.

He looked over my shoulder at Gabriel, as if for approval, and then approached the bed. Reaching out, he cupped my breasts.

Gabriel's thrusts rocked my nipples in and out of his hands.

I shuddered as Liam clamped them between his fingers. "God, that feels so good. More!"

Liam leaned down and took one of my nipples into his mouth. Then he suckled the sensitive peak.

The combined sensation of Gabriel thrusting and Liam sucking threw me right into an erotic abyss. I screamed as pleasure short-circuited my mind.

Gabriel thrust one more time and exploded inside me.

I orgasmed again—every muscle in my body tightening and releasing. Slowly, I grew aware of the fact that Gabriel had slipped out of my body and Liam sat on the bed holding me.

"I got you, beautiful," the giant rumbled.

I looked down at his huge cock and licked my lips. "Your turn."

Liam looked back at Gabriel, who'd collapsed at the other end of the bed. "Is she ready?"

He should ask me. I grabbed his chin and forced his gaze to mine. "She's very ready." Then I reached down and stroked his shaft.

Liam let out a ragged groan.

I slid my hand back and forth, marveling at the size. I tried to close my fingers around the throbbing length and failed. *It's so big.* I let out a throaty moan of appreciation.

He shuddered. "That feels amazing."

"This will feel even more amazing," I said, pushing him back on the bed and straddling him. "Take off your clothes."

"Okay," he gasped, yanking off his shirt and lifting me so he could kick off his pants.

I ran my fingers through his soft chest hair enjoying the differences between his huge hairy body and Gabriel's sleeker muscular one. Before I could continue my exploration, my core tightened with need and a wave of lust swept over me. *Can't wait.* I positioned myself over the blunt head of his cock.

He let out a hiss of breath.

Remembering that it was his first time, I slid down his cock slowly wanting him to savor the sensation.

Tendons strained in his neck as he fisted the bed sheets. His eyes glazed with desire.

Oh, God. Although I was drenched with passion and Gabriel's seed, I had to stop halfway down to let my body adjust to his incredible size.

Seeming to sense my discomfort, Liam grabbed my hips. "Stop. I don't want to hurt you."

"You're not hurting me." I leaned over and kissed him passionately.

His eyes fluttered shut, and he moaned against my lips.

I took advantage of his distraction to fully impale myself. My inner walls burned as his huge cock stretched me to the point of pain.

He let out a cry, his eyes flying open and staring straight into mine. His expression of dazed excitement thrilled me.

Gradually the sting between my legs ebbed leaving only

desire. Every one of my nerve endings came alive as I moved over him.

I'm his first. His last. The instinct to claim him overpowered me. "You're mine," I whispered.

The shocked expression that crossed his face was quickly replaced by joy. "Yes, yours," he echoed.

A bond snapped between us, and somehow I was feeling what he was feeling and hearing every thought in his head.

She claimed me! His chest swelled with happiness. *She claimed me!*

"Not quite yet," I whispered into his mind, rocking back on his magnificent cock.

"Ah, fuck." His eyes rolled back in his head.

Loving the way he filled every inch of me, I rode him hard. The pace I set was fast and furious and had our sweat-slicked bodies slapping together.

Shuddering, he surged up to meet my strokes, his hands cupping my breasts. "I'm close," he gasped.

Feeling his mounting desire through our bond, I slammed down harder. Molten heat raged inside me.

A guttural sound broke from his lips as he came. His orgasm ricocheted through me and sent me spiraling straight into an ocean of bliss.

Collapsing down on his chest in a boneless heap, I struggled to catch my breath.

Liam's thundering heartbeat drummed against my ear. "That was everything I hoped for," he said, kissing me on my forehead. "I'm glad you were the one."

A loud snore had me jerking my head up.

Gabriel lay a few feet away in a dead sleep.

"Seriously, brother? We're having a moment here." Liam threw a pillow at his friend's head.

Gabriel didn't stir.

I couldn't help giggling.

"You must've worn him out," Liam said, pulling me into the curve of his arm.

"He hasn't slept in days," Mason said in a low voice.

Mason! Shit. I'd forgotten all about the male. I looked over to see the gorgeous doctor leaning against the dresser.

He watched us with smoldering eyes, his nostrils flaring.

He wants me. My sex pulsed with a warm deep throb. *I could definitely go another round or two or three.*

"Then go another round with me," Liam said, kissing me.

I pushed him away. "No fair reading my mind."

"You've already learned how to speak telepathically?" Mason asked, pushing away from the dresser and coming to stand next to the bed. "It took me months to figure it out."

Liam brushed his hand through my hair. "She claimed me."

"Oh." Mason took a step back, a stunned expression on his face.

I looked between the men. "What do you mean by claimed? We had sex, like I had sex with Gabriel."

Liam shook his head. "It's more than that. When you told me I was yours and I agreed, our souls connected. We're now bonded for life. That's why you can read my mind so easily and why I can tell you are suddenly filled with panic."

I sat up in the bed feeling completely overwhelmed.

"Shh. It's okay," Liam whispered, rising up next to me. He leaned over and kissed my shoulder. "Don't be upset."

"She claimed you without knowing what she was doing?" Mason asked, sounding incredulous.

"Apparently, Doc."

Anxiety knotted my stomach. "What does it mean to be claimed?"

Liam wrapped his arms around me. "It means we're family now. I'll never leave your side as long as we live."

I searched his handsome face. "Really?"

Liam leaned over and kissed me. "Really. Unless you decide to break the bond, not even death can separate us."

Wow. My throat grew tight. My whole life I'd ached for this kind of connection. I wrapped my arms around Liam's neck and deepened the kiss. The minty taste of his lips made heat build between my legs. I moaned. *Again?* My body seemed insatiable.

Out of the corner of my eye, I saw Mason awkwardly pick an invisible piece of lint from his slacks. "Well, I should leave you two alone."

No way is he leaving. Now that I knew how to create a family, I planned on immediately expanding it. I broke away from Liam.

He tried to drag me back down on the bed.

I gently pushed away. *"Loving me means sharing."*

Although his disappointment came through our bond, he nodded in understanding. *"I know. Doc's turn."*

"Thank you," I whispered through our private connection. Then, I reached out and grabbed Mason's hand before he could walk away. "I could use another shower. How about you help me clean off with those magic hands of yours?"

20

MASON

All I could do was nod like an idiot when she pulled me into the bathroom. The sway of her heart-shaped bottom captivated me. *Have I ever seen a more perfect-looking ass?*

It should've bothered me that she'd just been with two other males, but somehow seeing her with them only inflamed my desire.

Her color was high as she dropped my hand and walked into the ridiculously large glass shower. She twisted the knob handle and water poured out of numerous showerheads mounted on the ceiling above. Giving me a seductive look, she grabbed a bar of soap from the bench and washed her body.

Mesmerized by her hands working the thick lather across her breasts and stomach, all rational thought left my brain.

Then she rubbed lower, sliding the soap between her legs.

"Bloody hell." My dick strained toward her, begging me to finish what we'd started earlier in the infirmary.

"Aren't you coming in?" she asked in a husky voice.

Hell, yes. Without another thought I pulled open the glass door and stepped in.

"Your clothes," she giggled.

"Oh." I look down at my wet pants and shirt. *Screw it. Who cares about clothes at a time like this?* I whipped my shirt over my head and shucked my pants and boxer shorts. As her gaze roamed my body, I couldn't help but feel self-conscious. Regular workouts and my Lykos physiology gave me a muscular body that would make any human proud, but I was still no match for the hulking males in the other room. Standing before her in the raw, while she'd just seen every inch of their bodies, did nothing for my ego.

As if sensing my anxiety, she traced a drop of water down my pectorals and then cupped my face in her hands. "You're perfect, Mason, and you're mine." She looked up at me with her beautiful golden gaze and suddenly it seemed as if she was peering into my soul.

"Yes, I'm yours, love," I answered, my heart exploding with emotions so intense they threatened to crush my sternum. All my life I'd been searching for this. To truly belong to something—someone. And now I belonged to her. My eyes stung as the bond snapped in place between us. *"You claimed me."*

"And now I need you to claim me," she whispered back into my mind. Her aching desire rushed through our bond.

She needs me. She needs this. I crushed my lips down on hers and devoured her moan.

She rocked back against me.

Our lips and tongue mated in a frenzied dance before I got control of myself. I needed to give her what the others hadn't. I needed to do more than just fuck her. Resolute, I pushed her back against the shower wall and dropped to my knees. Water sprayed my face and back, but I paid it no mind. All my attention was fixed on the center of her.

Her mouth made a sweet little O as I parted her thighs and moved one of her beautiful legs over my shoulder.

Then I delved into her with my lips and tongue—exploring her in a way none of the others had. Her honey-sweet flavor forever imprinted on my tongue. *I'll crave her taste forever.*

She screamed and rocked against my mouth. "Please, please," she begged.

Unable to resist her plea, I clamped my lips around her clitoris and sucked hard.

She convulsed in fits in spasms and sagged into my arms.

It was my turn to chuckle as I carried her over to the tile bench that stretched almost a third the length of the shower.

She looked up at me with hungry eyes as I positioned her on her back with her legs hanging off the end. "I need you inside me."

"I want to give you more pleasure," I said as I knelt down on the shower floor and nudged her thighs apart.

Water beat down on us as I slipped two fingers inside her and stroked her to a rhythm that had her writhing in ecstasy. Her desire radiated through our bond, amplifying my passion.

"Oh, God, Mason." She reached down and grabbed me.

The feel of her slick fingers moving up and down my throbbing erection destroyed my plan to make slow love to her. Trembling, I rose over her and thrust between her legs. *Bloody hell.* She was like a hot, wet vise clamping down on me.

Our bond magnified each movement. Her lust became mine and my passion became hers.

As she arched off the bench, pressure built inside me. Unable to help myself, I slammed into her harder and harder. Our wet bodies slid against each other under the spray of the hot water.

"Yes," she cried, anchoring her legs around my waist.

With her wrapped around me, I picked her up and carried

her to the middle of the shower. With my hands supporting her buttocks, and her back against the tile, I pounded into her giving her everything I had.

"Oh, Mason," she panted into my ear. She raked her nails down my shoulders as she took every thrust. "I'm so close."

I pulled back and angled my hips so the top of her mound scraped against me with every thrust.

She detonated in my arms.

I swallowed her cries of pleasure and surrendered to the vortex roaring inside me. My knees gave out with the power of my orgasm and I sank down to the shower floor with her in my arms. "Wow," I panted when I was capable of speech.

She burrowed her head into my neck. "Wow is right. Glad I saved the best for last."

I kissed her forehead, filled with so much emotion I couldn't hold back. "I'm falling in love with you, Havana."

She pulled away, her gaze searching mine. "You barely know me."

"I know that I could search the world over and not find another female as beautiful, smart, brave, and sexy as you." She was the one for me. *Now and forever*.

She smiled and pressed her body up against mine. "It's crazy as hell, but I'm falling for you too, Mason."

I'm not sure how long we lay there under the pouring water, but at some point we got out of the shower and toweled each other off.

What started off innocent turned into something far naughtier and moments later I was taking her on the bathroom counter.

When we'd both orgasmed again, I hugged her tightly. Part of me never wanted us to leave the bathroom, but the loud growl of her stomach made it clear she needed something to eat.

Wrapping the towels around us like togas, we opened the

bathroom door and stepped into the bedroom along with a cloud of steam.

"About damn time," Liam said. He stood with his arms crossed and his back resting against one of the bedposts. Thankfully, he'd put his pants back on. "I thought we were going to have to send in a search party."

Gabriel sat nude on the edge of the bed, his one-eyed gaze on Havana. "How are you feeling?"

"Hungry." Her cheeks, already flushed with the steam of the shower, grew redder. "I mean, hungry for actual food."

Remembering the lunch I'd made her, I rushed into the hallway and grabbed the tray. "I'm sorry, it's gotten a little cold."

Her eyes widened at the sight of the food. "That looks amazing. Thank you, Mason." She kissed my cheek as I set the tray down on a table next to a wingback chair.

"You can thank me by eating," I whispered into her mind. I took her hand and led her to the chair.

She gave me another look of appreciation as she dove into the chicken pasta and fruit salad. "This is delicious."

I couldn't help beaming with her praise. From now on, the purpose of my existence was to make her happy.

"Hey, I drove out to the cabin and picked up your things," Liam said, stomping out to the hallway and coming back with her duffel bag.

Havana's eyes lit up. "Thank you!"

She must've said something privately to Liam because he knelt next to her while she planted a kiss on his lips.

Needing to be closer to her, I leaned against the wall near where she sat.

Liam settled by her feet and we both watched her eat in silence.

"She claimed you both," Gabriel stated with a note of incredulousness in his voice. "I can't believe it."

"Believe it, brother," Liam said with a wide grin.

A shadow moved across Gabriel's face, but it passed so quickly, I could've imagined it. "Since you two can see to her needs, I'll head out." Gabriel strode toward the door. His jerky movements telegraphed his anger better than his brittle tone of voice.

Havana pushed her plate aside and stood up. "I want to claim you too, Gabriel."

Gabriel stopped and wheeled around. "That can't happen."

I felt her mood plummet through our bond.

"You don't want me," she said, blinking rapidly.

"He's a fool," I said, needing to soothe her hurt feelings.

A growl rumbled from Liam's throat, his need to protect her stirring too.

"No, fuck." Gabriel scrubbed a hand along the stubble on his chin. "There's nothing more I'd want in this world than to belong to you, but I won't weaken you or shorten your life." He scowled at Liam and me. "Did you not think of that when you accepted her claim?"

Damn. I'd been selfish. Regret stabbed into me like a scalpel.

Liam hung his head.

Havana threw up her hands. "Talk to me, guys. What am I missing here?"

Gabriel crossed the room to stand in front of her. "There's a reason why Alpha females never claim mates. Once bonded, when one mate dies so does the other. Unlike you and the other Alpha females, Liam, Mason, and I won't live extended lives. We'll grow old and die in the same life span humans have and if you're bound to us so will you." His words hung heavy in the air.

Havana shrugged. "So."

Gabriel blinked at her. "Don't you want to live for hundreds of years?"

Havana rose on the balls of her feet so she could meet Gabriel's penetrating stare. "What I want is to have a family. I want to live my life with you three. You're mine, Gabriel."

He shook his head. "No."

"Gabriel." His name was a plea on her lips.

His shoulders sagged and his resistance crumbled. "I'm yours," he whispered. His entire body shuddered, and I knew the bond between them was snapping in place.

I swatted back the surge of jealousy. *I'm hers too.*

She must've heard me because she broke away from Gabriel. She looked over at me and then down at Liam. "Yes, all three of you are mine."

We nodded in unison.

I studied the other two males. We were family now— connected through our bond with Havana. It wasn't the family I'd been searching for, but somewhere inside of me I knew it was the family I needed.

Our female reached up and removed Gabriel's eye patch.

I didn't know what private conversation they were having, but Gabriel shook his head.

Havana wrapped her arms around him. "It wasn't your fault. Don't let that bitch continue to torment you."

"Listen to her, brother," Liam said softly.

Gabriel reached a trembling hand up to the gemstone, but then froze. "I-I can't. Tasha's compulsion is too strong."

"Let me try to break it," Havana pleaded.

"Do it," Gabriel said, his body rigid with tension.

"Take the stone out, Gabriel!" Havana commanded, her voice ringing with Alpha power.

Clenching his teeth, Gabriel tore the jewel from his eye socket.

Despite the spurting blood and Gabriel's muffled groan, Havana didn't flinch or back away even when the male handed her the bloody gem and transformed into a brown wolf.

No sooner had his four paws hit the ground than he was taking his human form again.

I couldn't help but be impressed with his speed and control. I'd never seen anyone transform so fast. His position as head Enforcer was clearly well deserved.

Gabriel straightened his spine and opened two eyes. He smiled down at Havana, without the lines of tension that had marred his face as long as I'd known him. "You've made me whole."

She rose up on her toes and kissed his lips. "Now you need to do something for me." She looked over at Liam and me. "You all need to do something for me."

"Anything," our three voices echoed in the bedroom.

She let her towel drop to the floor. "Make love to me."

❈ 21 ❈

HAVANA

I woke caged between Liam and Gabriel, gasping for breath.

Gabriel's muscular chest pressed into my back while Liam's soft chest hair tickled my nose.

With Liam's muscular bicep draped over me, no wonder I felt like I was suffocating. Swallowing my laughter, I carefully scooted out from under his arm. Trying my best not to jar the men, I crawled to the edge of the bed and stepped onto the plush cashmere rug.

Although Liam frowned and moved his arm as if searching for my warmth, he stayed sleeping.

The most intimate parts of my body ached in ways they never had before. Without even making a conscious decision, I transformed into my wolf and back. Immediately, all my aches vanished, even the slight burn between my legs.

I blushed thinking of how the four of us had made love straight through the night. Each man had taken me one after another. We'd only broke occasionally for food. I trembled as the scandalous memories assaulted me. *Oh my!* I'd had more sex and in more different positions in the past twenty-four hours than I'd ever had in my life. *Except for the time with Nathan*, my inner voice corrected.

For the first time thinking of him didn't bring about a dull ache in my chest. *I'm over him*, I realized in surprise. Mating with Gabriel, Liam, and Mason had eased my pain and fused back together the pieces of my soul.

Smiling, I padded over to the dresser and searched the drawers until I found a white T-shirt. I held the soft cotton up to my nose inhaling the faint scent of sandalwood that would forever bring to mind my ex. The shirt was something Nathan would've likely worn under a button-down dress shirt, and something my new sexy mates would pair with jeans that I would slowly remove with my teeth.

Stop, shouted an inner voice. *What kind of madness would possess you to have sex with three different guys?* For a moment, shame and guilt rolled through me. With a shake of my head, I batted the feelings away. I refused to feel any regret for the naughty things I'd done last night and the even naughtier things I planned to do with my guys at the earliest opportunity. The old rules—the human rules, didn't apply anymore. A low rumbling growl escaped my lips as I pulled the shirt over my head. *I'm a freaking Alpha female werewolf and they're my mates*. I grinned as I looked over at Liam and Gabriel. Well, two of my mates anyway. *Where's Mason?*

He'd definitely gone to sleep with us. After my body's raging need for sex had finally ebbed, we'd all collapsed together on the mattress. Mason had lain at my feet, giving me the most relaxing foot rub before I'd passed out. *Maybe he's in the bathroom*. I peered inside, but the bathroom was empty.

My next guess was the kitchen. Mason had demonstrated impressive culinary skills several times over the past twenty-four hours. *What a catch*. I couldn't help grinning. They all were. Liam so gentle, but fiercely protective. Gabriel whose sexy dark edges couldn't overshadow his strength and loyalty. And Mason who—

The sight of the gorgeous blond doctor stepping into the room with a tray laden with food temporarily distracted me. The delicious aroma of coffee, bacon, and eggs had me inhaling deeply. *Mmm.*

Mason stopped when he caught sight of me standing in the middle of the room. He'd clearly been up for a while as it looked like he'd showered and dressed in a fresh polo and chinos before making breakfast. "Is everything okay?"

"Yes. I was just looking for you," I whispered back.

"I hope you brought some of that for us," Liam's loud voice boomed from the bed.

Gabriel opened his two beautiful dark eyes and looked over at the tray of food. "That smells amazing."

I couldn't help smiling at the deep relaxation I could feel radiating from Gabriel. When I'd coaxed him into ending Tasha's cruel punishment, I'd hoped to end his physical suffering. It was a bonus that much of his emotional pain seemed to have lifted too.

The bloodstained acorn-sized jewel that had tormented him for so long sat on top of the dresser next to the eye patch Gabriel would never wear again. As I glared at the stone, it sparkled in the sunlight streaming through the window. It didn't matter how beautiful it was, I was chucking that thing in the trash the first opportunity I got. Gabriel didn't need the reminder of what that evil bitch had forced him to do.

"Hey, hey!" Mason cried as Liam and Gabriel descended on the tray he was holding like a pack of wolves. "Make sure you leave some for Havana."

Both Enforcers froze and turned to look at me.

"Sorry," Liam mumbled through the strips of bacon hanging out of his mouth.

I laughed so hard at their guilty expressions, my eyes

watered. "Looks like you boys worked up one hell of an appetite."

"You can say that again," Gabriel said, with a wicked grin. He grabbed one of the coffee cups off the tray and brought it over to me. "How are you feeling this morning?"

"Good." As I took the cup, I couldn't help staring at his body. His gorgeous naked body. Feeling my face warm, I said, "Thank you. For yesterday, and, um, last night."

He leaned over and kissed me. "The pleasure was all mine, princess."

The warmth of his soft lips sent a tingle down my spine, but thankfully it didn't trigger the agonizing lust that had possessed me yesterday.

Mason pushed the tray into the dark-haired man's back. "She'd have a better morning if you let her eat. She's famished."

My stomach rumbled loudly as if to underscore his words.

"Hey," Mason yelled, as Liam reached over to grab another strip of bacon.

Laughing, Gabriel stepped back and let Mason herd me toward the wingback chair.

The doctor kept Liam at bay while I ate some of the eggs and bacon.

"I made some muffins too," Mason said, uncovering another plate.

"Thank you. This is so amazing, Mason. But you don't need to wait on me like this."

"But I like to," Mason said flashing me a heart-stopping grin.

"He's an Omega," Liam said, trying to snatch another piece of bacon from the tray.

Mason smacked his hand with a snarl. "Omega or not, I'll still put you in your place if I have to. Wait until she finishes."

I shook my head as I sipped some of the delicious dark coffee. "What's an Omega?"

"The most submissive of us," Liam said, looking longingly at the tray. "Lykos are either Alphas, like you, Betas like us—" he waved between himself and Gabriel "—or Omegas like Doc here."

"Oh," I said, looking at Mason with new eyes.

Mason briefly met my stare and then lowered his gaze. "It's in my nature to care for you and the others."

"And it's in my nature to fight and protect what's mine," Liam added giving me a wolfish grin.

"So what is in the Alpha's nature?" I asked, curiosity getting the better of me.

"Leading their faction," Gabriel called out from across the room. "Or in Tasha's case, killing her enemies, inflicting pain on the weak, and torturing Lykos and humans for sport."

What a nasty bitch. I hoped I'd never encountered her again, but if I did, I'd do everything in my power to destroy her. *Assuming she doesn't destroy me first.* The last bite of muffin turned to ash in my mouth. I managed to swallow it down and then set my plate on the tray. "You can have the rest," I said to Liam. When Mason shot me an anxious look, I patted my stomach. "I couldn't eat another thing."

Liam gleefully grabbed the tray, carried it to the bed, and dove into it as if he hadn't had a meal in weeks.

"You should grab something before he inhales it all," I called out to Gabriel who stared out the window with a pensive look on his face.

He shook his head. "The storm broke last night. We were so...distracted, we didn't notice."

I stood and walked over to his side. The view was breathtaking. Outside, there wasn't a cloud in the bright blue sky and a thick blanket of glittery snow covered the ground and all the pine trees in every direction. *It looks like a winter fairy-*

land. Happiness bubbled up inside me like champagne. "This will be my first white Christmas," I exclaimed, reaching out and clasping Gabriel's hand.

He brought my hand to his lips, the rough stubble on his jaw gently scraping my knuckles.

"Then we should make it the best Christmas you've ever had," Mason said, coming up behind me. He wrapped his long tanned arms around my waist and settled his clean-shaven face on the curve of my neck.

Smiling, I nuzzled Mason's golden hair marveling at its softness.

If anything, Gabriel's expression darkened. Through our bond, I could feel the worry gnawing at him.

"What's wrong, Gabriel?"

"Nathan will come," he said solemnly. "The storm has passed. There's nothing keeping him away now."

"Good. I can't wait to see Mira again." I smiled thinking of the little spitfire and how she'd wrap my mates around her pinkie finger in no time.

"He'll be pissed about this." Gabriel motioned between the four of us.

I shrugged. "He can deal. We're together and there's nothing Nathan can do to change that."

Gabriel pressed his lips together, but he couldn't keep me from his thoughts. *"She loves him. When he comes, she may decide she wants him. Not us."*

I squeezed his hand. *"I loved Nathan. He's the past. You, Liam, and Mason are my future."*

"Damn straight," Liam said, joining our mental chat. He strode over to the window and reached for my free hand. *"If he challenges us we'll lay the hurt down, right, Gabe?"*

The head Enforcer answered with a fierce baring of his teeth. "Hell, yeah."

"Havana is ours, and we are hers, forever," Mason added,

tightening his grip around my waist. "Now, back to a much more important topic. What do you want for Christmas, love?"

With Gabriel holding my right hand, Liam holding my left hand, and Mason's arms wrapped snug around me, I sighed with contentment. "I can't think of a single thing."

Liam rubbed his beard for a moment and then gave me a wicked grin. "Well, I have some ideas."

I arched an eyebrow. "Oh really. Like what?"

Liam didn't say anything, but gave a knowing glance to Mason and Gabriel.

"Great idea, brother. Why don't we all go and check out that walk-in shower?" Gabriel tugged me toward the bathroom.

Mason let the dark-haired man pull me out of his arms. "Excellent plan. Dibs on the bench."

Laughing the four of us rushed toward the door. It was hours before we emerged, wet, flushed from the hot water, and very, very satisfied.

THANKS FOR READING

If you enjoyed this book please leave a review on Amazon or any other reader site or blog you frequent. I prioritize continuing series based on the reviews I receive so if you would like to see more of Havana and her sexy mates let me know!

The adventure continues!

CLAIMING HER MATES: BOOK TWO

Once she saves his life, he'll have hell to pay...

Riding out the apocalypse with my sexy mates in a luxurious mountain lodge sounds like a dream. But for some asinine reason, Liam, Mason, and Gabriel have adopted a hands-off policy.

Even worse, my ex hasn't met up with us as promised. If sexual frustration doesn't kill me, my growing anxiety over the missing Alpha male might.

The only solution is to teach my mates a scorching lesson in satisfying my needs and launch a rescue mission. Nathan may have betrayed me and broken my heart, but I won't let him die. At least not until I've given him a piece of my mind...

ABOUT THE AUTHOR

Dia wanted to be a writer from the time she could hold a pencil. A lover of paranormal romance, reverse harem, science fiction, urban fantasy, and horror, she writes action-packed stories featuring kick-butt heroines and the alpha male heroes who fall for them.

If you want to be notified when the next book in the series releases please sign up for my newsletter on my website.

https://diacole.com/

EXCERPT FROM CLAIMING HER MATES: BOOK TWO

1

HAVANA

A shot of adrenaline spiked my blood as two giant wolves tried to bring me down. The silvery-white snow crunched like broken glass under my paws.

Gabriel, the dark brown wolf, stayed on my left flank, while Liam, the massive russet-colored wolf, pressed in on my right.

"Stop, Havana!" Gabriel telepathically ordered. *"We're almost at the wall."*

As if his words conjured it up, the eighteen-foot stone wall that protected Sanctuary, the forty-acre property where we were riding out the apocalypse, appeared in the distance.

Almost there. I increased my pace.

"Enough!" Gabriel shouted into my mind. *"You know the rules. Stop!"*

"It's not safe," Liam added.

I was sick of safe. I was sick of pacing the floors of the luxurious winter lodge pretending the world wasn't imploding. But most of all, I was sick of them treating me like a fragile doll that could shatter at any moment. It'd been a week since either of them had touched me. I gnashed my teeth in frustration.

I might have tolerated the lack of intimacy better had it not been Christmas Eve, the anniversary of my mother's death.

Remembering my mom brought back bittersweet memories. She'd been MIA most of my childhood, but she'd been the only family I'd had. Scratch that, I had a new family. One I'd created by claiming the sexiest three guys I'd ever met.

One of those guys was back at the lodge trying to find a cure for the Z-virus using his medical expertise. The other two were hot on my heels.

Seeming to realize I wasn't stopping, Gabriel and Liam both rushed forward and tried to tackle me to the ground. But I was too fast. In a burst of speed, I darted past them and bounded over the wall in a single physics-defying leap.

Crunch.

I landed in the middle of a snowdrift, the soft impact not slowing me in the slightest. With a toss of my muzzle, I shook off the feathery flakes and continued loping down the road. In just minutes, I came to a small run-down cabin.

Funny how a little more than a week ago, I'd risked death itself to escape that place. Of course I'd been dying of the zombie-plague so braving a snowstorm to seek help from Mason, Liam, and Gabriel seemed the lesser of two evils.

Thankfully, Mason had cured me and sent me into my first werewolf transformation. That triggered my first heat cycle, which resulted in me claiming him, Gabriel, and Liam as my own.

My breath came faster as I remembered all the ways my sexy mates and me had mated. It'd been incredible. The scorching memory of our foursome in the shower kept me from sleeping most nights. I physically ached for more. But my mates apparently didn't feel the same. I'd done everything

I could to stir their interest including become a nudist around the lodge, and still they kept me at arm's length.

Never in my life had I been this needy. It was as if my Lykos transformation had flipped me into some kind of sexual hyperdrive. The sexual frustration along with the mounting anxiety each day that my ex, Nathan, and his young daughter didn't arrive was driving me insane.

My heart ached as I thought of little Mira, who I used to nanny. She and her father should have been at Sanctuary ten days ago, but there had been no sign of them and, without working cell towers, we had no way of contacting them. For all I knew they hadn't even made it out of Saguaro Valley, one of the epicenters of the outbreak.

They could've been attacked. My stomach churned at the thought of Mira being hurt or worse. Her father, on the other hand, could become zombie food for all I cared. Three months ago, the rat bastard had ripped my heart out and stomped all over it when he'd kissed his supposed dead wife in front of me. To add insult to injury, Nathan proceeded to tell me our relationship had meant nothing to him right before he slammed his front door in my face.

All those times he'd told me he loved me. *Lies.* All those plans we'd made. *More lies.* Nathan's betrayal had shattered my naïve belief in love and happily-ever-afters. The only good to come out of that experience was I'd learned how to claw myself out of the depths of depression, and Nathan had, in a roundabout way, introduced me to my mates.

Although Gabriel had tried to convince me that Nathan might have ended our relationship to save me from Tasha, the vicious Alpha of Winterhaven, I didn't entirely buy it. Nathan had been too cold. Too cruel that night. And that kiss he'd given Tasha had looked plenty real to me.

I growled as Tasha's model-perfect face came to mind. *Fuck her.* It didn't help that my mates were fixated on her too.

They all seemed to live in fear of her arrival. Sanctuary was her vacation home and my mates were supposed to be her loyal subjects. Apparently, the statuesque blonde would murder us all on sight for taking what was hers.

I snorted. *Let her try.* The psychotic bitch had forced Gabriel to kill his own family and tortured him for years afterward. I looked forward to avenging his pain.

The sound of panting breaths made my heart race. *They're gaining on me. Can't let them catch me...yet.*

With a single bound, I landed on the rickety wooden steps of the cabin and immediately took my human form. The first few times I'd reshaped my body had been disorienting. However, after practice, shape-shifting had become second nature, just like the ability to shield my thoughts from my mates. Thrilled they'd have no idea what I had in store for them, I yanked the front door open.

The sharp, sweet scent of the peppermint oil Liam had used to drive off the former furry occupants of the cabin beckoned me inside. The cozy interior, with the large windows overlooking the frozen river out back, was almost the same as I'd remembered. Of course, the fire in the woodstove had gone out. But it wasn't as if my bare skin even registered the cold. One of the many perks of being a Lykos.

Sitting across from the rocking chair and leather recliner was the bed where I hoped the next stage of my plan would land me.

My favorite boots, black dress, and long charcoal wool jacket lay on the soft white cashmere area rug next to an IV stand. Mason must've taken off my wet clothes to warm me the night he found me freezing outside. I wrinkled my nose at the sight of the coagulated bag of blood still attached to the pole. *Ugh. Tasha's blood.* Although a transfusion of her blood had healed and transformed me into a rare and powerful Alpha female, it made me sick to think some part of that monstrous woman was running through my veins.

Deciding that the IV stand was a mood killer, I walked in, grabbed it, and wheeled it to the far corner of the cabin. Then I hid it behind the curtain Mason had hung around a bedpan. Thank God, I'd been able to upgrade my accommodations before I'd been forced to use the makeshift bathroom. I'd never take running water and electricity for granted again.

The sound of stomping feet on the wood steps outside was my only warning before the cabin door flew open and a scowling, naked, dark-haired man stormed inside.

Gabriel's eyes glinted with anger. "Havana, what's the meaning of this?" His ragged breathing brought my attention to the smooth bronze muscles of his chest.

Unable to help myself, my gaze dipped lower to his six-pack abs, and then even lower to the delicious package hanging between his legs. I bit back my moan. I couldn't wait to lick, suck, and bite every delicious inch of his powerful body. Playing dumb, I batted my eyelashes. "Are you upset about something?"

He ran a hand through his collar-length hair. "Fuck yeah, I'm upset. You know you need to stay behind the wall."

He looks so sexy when he's agitated. "Then it sounds like you need to punish me for breaking the rules." I knocked several pillows aside and crawled onto the bed. "Do you want to spank me?" I twisted around to present him with my naked bottom. Although as an exotic dancer I'd played at being a BDSM queen on stage, I'd discovered that I loved being dominated in bed.

No one dominated better than Gabriel. *Except Nathan*, a wicked voice inside my head whispered. I bitch-slapped that unwelcome commentary and focused on the dark-haired male.

Gabriel clenched his jaw. "Don't tempt me."

But that's exactly what I planned on doing. I gave Gabriel a coy look through my long dark hair. "If you don't correct me now, I might have to run away again and again..."

"Havana." His rumbling warning would've made any sane woman back down.

But mounting sexual frustration made me a bit crazy. "You should spank me."

He growled. His growing lust pulsed through our bond.

He wants me. Then why won't he give us what we both crave?

When he didn't move a muscle. I chewed on my lower lip. "Well, if you aren't man enough to give me the punishment I deserve then maybe—" I broke off when he crossed the distance between us in a blur of motion.

"You forget, I'm not a man at all," he growled, grabbing my hips.

Yes! "Take me," I pleaded, spreading my thighs. Rough. Gentle. Fast. Slow. I didn't care as long as he quenched this burning ache inside me. I rocked back feeling the scorching heat of his erection against my core.

He inhaled sharply and took a step back. "Princess, I can't."

"Why the hell not?" We'd already overcome his initial reluctance to mate with me because he'd thought of me as Nathan's female. *What's his hang-up now?*

"We don't want to hurt the babe," a deep, rumbling voice said from the doorway.

I looked around Gabriel's shoulder to see a gorgeous seven-foot-tall, auburn-haired, bearded male. "What baby?"

Liam strode in and shut the cabin door behind him. "The babe you're carrying."

Gabriel nodded. "It's important you take it easy right now. As much as I—" he looked over at Liam "—as much as we want to be with you, we don't want to jeopardize the pregnancy." He looked down at his bare wrist as if checking an imaginary watch. "We should get back to the lodge. Mason will have lunch ready by now. A female in your condition needs to eat regularly. Lykos pregnancies aren't like human pregnancies. The gestation takes less than half the time and is very demanding on the mothers."

I shook my head in disbelief. *They can't be serious?* I flipped over on my back and stared at the two of them. "I'm not pregnant. I have an IUD."

Gabriel's eyes widened. "You do?"

"Hell yeah, I do." I'd had the procedure done when Nathan and I first got together. All my life I'd wanted children, but I'd wanted them after I was married. I'd promised myself early in life that I'd never end up in my mother's shoes —partnerless and raising an unplanned child.

My stomach tightened as I thought of my mom again. Even though she and I had a complicated relationship, I missed her.

Liam strode over the wood floor and came to stand next to Gabriel. "What's an IUD?"

"I think it's a form of birth control," Gabriel answered slowly.

I sighed. Explaining contraception to werewolves was one of many conversations I never thought I'd have. "It's a device implanted inside my body that prevents me from getting pregnant."

"But you went into heat?" Liam said, looking confused.

I shrugged. "That wouldn't matter. I can't get pregnant until the IUD is removed." I'm sure when the time came, Mason would be more than happy to do the honors.

"But...but... Don't you want babes?" Liam asked, his gaze searching my face.

"Very much," I answered honestly. But I wanted it to be a planned event. My mom never let me forget I was a not so appreciated parting gift from a one-night stand. "Just not right now." Bringing a baby into the apocalypse wouldn't be the smartest idea even if the child would have some amazing daddies to look after him or her.

"So you're not pregnant," Liam said, his green eyes darkening.

"She's not pregnant," Gabriel echoed, reaching down to caress my breast.

"Not even a little." I moaned and arched into his hand. My nipple instantly hardened into a tight nub. "So are you two going to punish me for breaking the rules?"

"Hell, yes we are." Gabriel pinched my sensitive peak with enough pressure to take my breath away.

"You've been a very naughty female." Liam pinched my other nipple.

"Oh!" I gasped brokenly at the pleasure-pain sensation. My heart pounded with anticipation as I swept my gaze over the gorgeous naked males in front of me. It'd been so long and I needed this. I needed them.

2

HAVANA

Pushing Liam's hand away, Gabriel grabbed hold of my ankles and dragged me to the edge of the bed. He pushed my legs apart and brushed his thumb lightly over my sex.

I moaned and bucked against his touch.

"Look how hungry she is for us, Liam. She's already dripping wet." Gabriel slid two fingers inside me.

I whimpered at the erotic invasion. It felt so good.

Liam licked his lips and watched Gabriel's fingers thrusting in and out of my damp flesh. "She likes that?"

"She likes it very much," I panted. I rocked up off the chocolate-colored comforter, chasing Gabriel's fingers.

Gabriel clamped his free hand on my hip, locking me in place. "None of that. You take what I give you—nothing more. Understand?" He pulled his fingers out, reached up, and pinched my nipple.

"Yes," I hissed, my eyes rolling back in my head. "Please." The agonizing throb between my legs had me shifting restlessly.

Gabriel looked over at his friend. "Watch and learn, brother. Our Alpha doesn't like it slow. Does she?" He slid three fingers in, and increased his tempo.

I cried out my approval. I loved the raw ferocity of Gabriel's lovemaking. He didn't do slow and sensuous like Mason. There was also never any sweet hesitancy to his touch like Liam. Gabriel fucked hard and raw. And right now that was exactly what I needed.

A savage hunger gripped me as I checked out the heavy muscles rippling under his dark bronze skin. *He's so goddamn hot.* I dropped my gaze to the heavy erection swinging between his thighs. I couldn't wait to feel his cock hammering deep inside me. And Liam's. I couldn't help but do a double take at Liam's massive erection. I grew wetter just thinking about fitting all of him inside me.

"Look at me, not Liam," Gabriel ordered.

A shiver went through me. I loved when Gabriel was bossy like this. *Nathan used to*—I crushed that thought before it could grow wings. Nathan was my past. Gabriel, Liam, and Mason were my present and future. I raised my gaze to meet Gabriel's.

"Good girl." His dark eyes blazed with wicked passion. "Do you want me to fuck you?"

"Yes." *So damn much.*

Gabriel pressed the head of his cock right where I needed it. "You want this inside you?" He dragged his hot, rigid flesh over my seam.

"Oh, God. Yes," I cried, rocking my hips forward.

"Then as part of your punishment, I won't fuck you." He pulled his hand and cock away.

"What? That's not fair." I tried to sit up.

"I say what's fair." Gabriel pushed me down. "Don't move unless I give you permission." He clamped his fingers around my clit.

Pleasure sizzled through my nerve endings. I arched off the mattress.

"Liam, how else should we punish this naughty female?" Gabriel gave my clit another pinch.

Liam's gaze lit up and he grinned at Gabriel.

Gabriel nodded in response to some silent telepathic conversation they were having. "Good idea." Then Gabriel climbed onto the bed. Before I could process what was happening, Gabriel pushed me into a seated position, with my legs hanging off the bed, and situated himself behind me.

I could feel his hard-as-steel cock against my ass. *Is he going to take me from behind?* "What's going on?"

"That's for us to know and you to find out." He reached around and clamped my nipples with his fingers.

I writhed in pleasure.

Liam got down on his knees in front of me. Despite his imposing size, he looked almost bashful. "I've always wanted to do this." He dipped his head down and kissed my knee. The whiskers of his beard brushed against the soft skin of my inner thigh.

I giggled.

Liam snapped his head up, looking confused.

I immediately bit my lip. *Poor guy.* He thought I was laughing at him.

"She's ticklish," Gabriel said to Liam. "But she won't laugh anymore, will she?" He twisted my nipples hard enough that I saw stars.

"No, I promise," I moaned.

"Keep going, brother," Gabriel ordered.

Liam blew a hot breath over my aching flesh. "Does this feel good?"

"Yes," I gasped, my entire body trembling.

"And this?" He pushed his face between my legs and licked.

The hot lash of his tongue on my sensitive flesh was so good it almost bordered on painful. "Oh, yes!"

Liam gave me a big smile. "You taste so sweet. I could do this forever."

"Make her beg for release." Gabriel tweaked my nipples again. "You're not allowed to orgasm until I say so, princess. Understand?"

"Y-yes," I gasped, wondering how the hell I was going to hold myself back.

Liam dove in, licking and sucking me senseless. Although he devoured my pussy with more enthusiasm than finesse, it was goddamn perfect.

My head fell back against Gabriel's chest as I gave myself over to the hot, wet friction of his mouth and tongue. Pleasure coiled tight inside me. I dug my nails into the side of Gabriel's thighs and held on to him for dear life.

"Here's another tip, brother." Gabriel reached down and spread my lips. "See that nub, that's her clit. Suck on it. "

Liam immediately drew my clit into his mouth eliciting a strangled moan from my lips.

Sizzling arcs of electricity pulsed through me. "I can't take much more!" My thighs trembled as I fought to hold back my orgasm.

"Oh, you'll take it," Gabriel growled into my ear. Then he looked down at Liam. "Fuck her with your tongue."

Liam spread my thighs wider and thrust his tongue deep inside me.

"Oh!" Erotic pleasure overwhelmed my senses. Gritting my teeth I tried to fight the mounting tension in my body.

Gabriel reached between us and pinched my clit.

It was too much. Liam's mouth. Gabriel's fingers. Blinding pleasure consumed me. I came hard, shaking between the two men like a rag doll.

When I'd finally stopped quivering from the aftershocks, Gabriel made a tsking sound. "You didn't take your punishment, princess. Now we'll have to punish you some more."

I licked my lips, my breath going choppier. *I can't wait...*

DID YOU ENJOY THIS PREVIEW?

You can find the book here: https://
mybook.to/ClaimingHerMates

Please don't forget to leave a review if you enjoyed this work!

Thank you for reading!

www.ingramcontent.com/pod-product-compliance
Lightning Source LLC
Chambersburg PA
CBHW050528190726
48284CB00003B/990